A World of Winnie-the-Pooh

A.A.MILNE

with illustrations by E.H.SHEPARD

A collection of stories, verse and hums
about the Bear of Very Little Brain

METHUEN CHILDREN'S BOOKS

First published in Great Britain in 1998
Produced in 1998 for W.H.Smith Limited
by Methuen Children's Books
an imprint of Egmont Children's Books Limited
Michelin House, 81 Fulham Road, London SW3 6RB
Copyright © 1998 by Michael John Brown, Peter Janson-Smith
Roger Hugh Vaughan Charles Morgan and
Timothy Michael Robinson, Trustees of the Pooh Properties.

Stories, verse and hums selected from
Winnie-the-Pooh, first published 14 October 1926
Text by A. A. Milne and line illustrations by E. H. Shepard
copyright under the Berne Convention.
Colouring of the illustrations copyright © 1970
by Ernest H. Shepard and Methuen and Co Ltd.
and copyright © 1973 by Ernest H. Shepard
and Methuen Children's Books Ltd.

The House at Pooh Corner, first published 11 October 1928
Text by A. A. Milne and line illustrations by E. H. Shepard
copyright under the Berne Convention.
Colouring of the illustrations copyright © 1970
by Ernest H. Shepard and Methuen and Co Ltd.
and © 1974 by Ernest H. Shepard and
Methuen Children's Books Ltd.

When We Were Very Young, first published 1924
Text by A. A. Milne and line illustrations by E. H. Shepard
copyright under the Berne Convention.
Colouring of the illustrations by Mark Burgess
copyright © 1989 by Egmont Children's Books Limited.

Now We Are Six, first published 1927
Text by A. A. Milne and line illustrations by E. H. Shepard
copyright under the Berne Convention.
Colouring of the illustrations by Mark Burgess
copyright © 1989 by Egmont Children's Books Limited.

Compiled by Susan Hitches
Cover design by Ania Mochlinska
copyright © 1989 by Egmont Children's Books Limited.

3 5 7 9 10 8 6 4 2

Printed and Bound in Italy

ISBN 0 416 19620 9

Contents

Winnie-the-Pooh and Some Bees 9

Happiness 25

Lines and Squares 26

Pooh Goes Visiting and gets into a Tight Place 27

Teddy Bear 36

Eeyore has a Birthday 42

Buckingham Palace 54

Kanga and Baby Roo Come to the Forest 56

Hoppity 68

A Thought 69

Piglet is Entirely Surrounded by Water 70

Down by the Pond 82

Christopher Robin Gives a Party 84

Waiting at the Window 96

Vespers 97

A House is Built for Eeyore 98

Sneezles 112

Furry Bear 115

Tigger Comes to the Forest and has Breakfast 116

Rice Pudding 128

Tiggers Don't Climb Trees 130

Halfway Down 145

Rabbit has a Busy Day 146

Us Two 158

Knight in Armour 161

Pooh Invents a New Game 162

The Engineer 174

Tigger is Unbounced 176

Spring Morning 188

Piglet Does a Very Grand Thing 190

Wind on the Hill 202

Solitude 203

An Enchanted Place 204

The Charcoal-Burner 218

The Friend 220

Winnie-the-Pooh and Some Bees

Here is Edward Bear, coming downstairs now, bump, bump, bump, on the back of his head, behind Christopher Robin. It is, as far as he knows, the only way of coming downstairs, but sometimes he feels that there really is another way, if only he could stop bumping for a moment and think of it. And then he feels that perhaps there isn't. Anyhow, here he is at the bottom, and ready to be introduced to you. Winnie-the-Pooh.

When I first heard his name, I said, just as you are going to say, "But I thought he was a boy?"

"So did I," said Christopher Robin.

"Then you can't call him Winnie?"

"I don't."

"But you said —"

"He's Winnie-ther-Pooh. Don't you know what '*ther*' means?"

"Ah, yes, now I do," I said quickly; and I hope you do too, because it is all the explanation you are going to get.

Sometimes Winnie-the-Pooh likes a game of some sort when he comes downstairs, and sometimes he likes to sit quietly in front of the fire and listen to a story. This evening —

"What about a story?" said Christopher Robin.

"*What* about a story?" I said.

"Could you very sweetly tell Winnie-the-Pooh one?"

"I suppose I could," I said. "What sort of stories does he like?"

"About himself. Because he's *that* sort of Bear."

"Oh, I see."

"So could you very sweetly?"

"I'll try," I said.

So I tried.

Once upon a time, a very long time ago now, about last Friday, Winnie-the-Pooh lived in a forest all by himself under the name of Sanders.

("What does 'under the name' mean?" asked Christopher Robin.

"It means he had the name over the door in gold letters and lived under it."

"Winnie-the-Pooh wasn't quite sure," said Christopher Robin.

"Now I am," said a growly voice.

"Then I will go on," said I.)

One day when he was out walking, he came to an open place in the middle of the forest, and in the middle of this place was a large oak-tree, and, from the top of the tree, there came a loud buzzing-noise.

Winnie-the-Pooh sat down at the foot of the tree, put his head between his paws, and began to think.

First of all he said to himself: "That buzzing-noise means something. You don't get a buzzing-noise like that, just buzzing and buzzing, without its meaning something. If there's a buzzing-noise, somebody's making a buzzing-noise, and the only reason for making a buzzing-noise that *I* know of is because you're a bee."

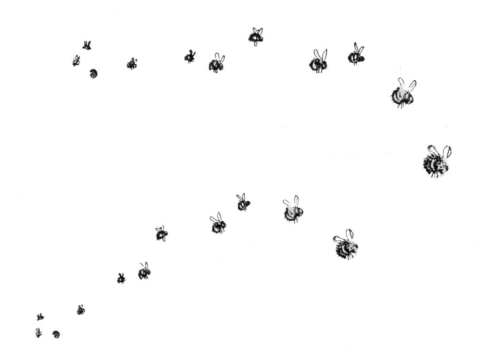

Then he thought another long time, and said: "And the only reason for being a bee that I know of is making honey."

And then he got up, and said: "And the only reason for making honey is so as *I* can eat it." So he began to climb the tree.

He
climbed
and
he
climbed
and
he
climbed,
and
as
he
climbed
he
sang
a
little
song
to
himself.
It
went
like
this:

Isn't it funny
How a bear likes honey?
Buzz! Buzz! Buzz!
I wonder why he does?

Then he climbed a little further . . . and a little further . . . and then just a little further. By that time he had thought of another song.

> It's a very funny thought that, if Bears were Bees,
> They'd build their nests at the *bottom* of trees.
> And that being so (if the Bees were Bears),
> We shouldn't have to climb up all these stairs.

He was getting rather tired by this time, so that is why he sang a Complaining Song. He was nearly there now, and if he just stood on that branch . . .

Crack!

"Oh, help!" said Pooh, as he dropped ten feet on to the branch below him.

"If only I hadn't —" he said, as he bounced twenty feet on to the next branch.

"You see, what I *meant* to do," he explained, as he turned head-over-heels, and crashed on to another branch thirty feet below, "what I *meant* to do —"

"Of course, it *was* rather —" he admitted, as he slithered very quickly through the next six branches.

"It all comes, I suppose," he decided, as he said good-bye to the last branch, spun round three times, and flew gracefully into a gorse-bush, "it all comes of *liking* honey so much. Oh, help!"

He crawled out of the gorse-bush, brushed the prickles from his nose, and began to think again. And the first person he thought of was Christopher Robin.

(*"Was that me?" said Christopher Robin in an awed voice, hardly daring to believe it.*

"That was you."

Christopher Robin said nothing, but his eyes got larger and larger, and his face got pinker and pinker.)

So Winnie-the-Pooh went round to his friend Christopher Robin, who lived behind a green door in another part of the Forest.

"Good morning, Christopher Robin," he said.

"Good morning, Winnie-*ther*-Pooh," said you.

"I wonder if you've got such a thing as a balloon about you?"

"A balloon?"

"Yes, I just said to myself coming along: 'I wonder if Christopher Robin has such a thing as a balloon about him?' I just said it to myself, thinking of balloons, and wondering."

"What do you want a balloon for?" you said.

Winnie-the-Pooh looked round to see that nobody was listening, put his paw to his mouth, and said in a deep whisper: *"Honey!"*

"But you don't get honey with balloons!"

"I do," said Pooh.

Well, it just happened that you had been to a party the day before at the house of your friend Piglet, and you had balloons at the party. You had had a big green balloon; and one of Rabbit's relations had had a big blue one, and had left it behind, being really too young to go to a party at all; and so you had brought the green one *and* the blue one home with you.

"Which one would you like?" you asked Pooh.

He put his head between his paws and thought very carefully.

"It's like this," he said. "When you go after honey with a balloon, the great thing is not to let the bees know you're coming. Now, if you have a green balloon, they might think you were only part of the tree, and not notice you, and if you have a blue balloon, they might think you were only part of the sky, and not notice you, and the question is: Which is most likely?"

"Wouldn't they notice *you* underneath the balloon?" you asked.

"They might or they might not," said Winnie-the-Pooh. "You never can tell with bees." He thought for a moment and said: "I shall try to look like a small black cloud. That will deceive them."

"Then you had better have the blue balloon," you said; and so it was decided.

Well, you both went out with the blue balloon, and you took your gun with you, just in case, as you always did, and Winnie-the-Pooh went to a

very muddy place that he knew of, and rolled and rolled until he was black all over; and then, when the balloon was blown up as big as big, and you and Pooh were both holding on to the string, you let go suddenly, and Pooh Bear floated gracefully up into the sky, and stayed there – level with the top of the tree and about twenty feet away from it.

"Hooray!" you shouted.

"Isn't that fine?" shouted Winnie-the-Pooh down to you. "What do I look like?"

"You look like a Bear holding on to a balloon," you said.

"Not," said Pooh anxiously, " – not like a small black cloud in a blue sky?"

"Not very much."

"Ah, well, perhaps from up here it looks different. And, as I say, you never can tell with bees."

There was no wind to blow him nearer to the tree so there he stayed. He could see the honey, he could smell the honey, but he couldn't quite reach the honey.

After a little while he called down to you.

"Christopher Robin!" he said in a loud whisper.

"Hallo!"

"I think the bees *suspect* something!"

"What sort of thing?"

"I don't know. But something tells me that they're *suspicious*!"

"Perhaps they think that you're after their honey?"

"It may be that. You never can tell with bees."

There was another little silence, and then he called down to you again.

"Christopher Robin!"

"Yes?"

"Have you an umbrella in your house?"

"I think so."

"I wish you would bring it out here, and walk up and down with it, and look up at me every now and then, and say 'Tut-tut, it looks like rain.' I think, if you did that, it would help the deception which we are practising on these bees."

Well, you laughed to yourself, "Silly old Bear!" but you didn't say it aloud because you were so fond of him, and you went home for your umbrella.

"Oh, there you are!" called down Winnie-the-Pooh, as soon as you got back to the tree. "I was beginning to get anxious. I have discovered that the bees are now definitely Suspicious."

"Shall I put my umbrella up?" you said.

"Yes, but wait a moment. We must be practical. The important bee to deceive is the Queen Bee. Can you see which is the Queen Bee from down there?"

"No."

"A pity. Well, now, if you walk up and down with your umbrella, saying, 'Tut-tut, it looks like rain,' I shall do what I can by singing a little Cloud Song, such as a cloud might sing. . . . Go!"

So, while you walked up and down and wondered if it would rain, Winnie-the-Pooh sang this song:

> How sweet to be a Cloud
>   Floating in the Blue!
> Every little cloud
> *Always* sings aloud.
>
> "How sweet to be a Cloud
>   Floating in the Blue!"
> It makes him very proud
> To be a little cloud.

The bees were still buzzing as
suspiciously as ever. Some of them,
indeed, left their nests and flew
all round the cloud as it
began the second verse of
this song, and one bee sat
down on the nose of the cloud for
a moment, and then got up again.

"Christopher – *ow!* – Robin,"
called out the cloud.

"Yes?"

"I have just been thinking, and I have come
to a very important decision. *These are the wrong
sort of bees.*"

"Are they?"

"Quite the wrong sort. So I should think they would make the wrong sort
of honey, shouldn't you?"

"Would they?"

"Yes. So I think I shall come down."

"How?" asked you.

Winnie-the-Pooh hadn't thought about this. If he let go of the string, he
would fall – *bump* – and he didn't like the idea of that.
So he thought for a long time, and then he said:

"Christopher Robin, you must shoot the
balloon with your gun. Have you got your gun?"

"Of course I have," you said. "But if I do that,
it will spoil the balloon," you said.

"But if you *don't*," said Pooh, "I shall have to
let go, and that would spoil *me*."

When he put it like this, you saw how it was,
and you aimed very carefully at the balloon,
and fired.

"*Ow!*" said Pooh.

"Did I miss?" you asked.

"You didn't exactly *miss*," said Pooh, "but you missed the *balloon.*"

"I'm so sorry," you said, and you fired again, and this time you hit the balloon, and the air came slowly out, and Winnie-the-Pooh floated down to the ground.

But his arms were so stiff from holding on to the string of the balloon all that time that they stayed up straight in the air for more than a week, and whenever a fly came and settled on his nose he had to blow it off. And I think – but I am not sure – that *that* is why he was always called Pooh.

"Is that the end of the story?" asked Christopher Robin.

"That's the end of that one. There are others."

"About Pooh and Me?"

"And Piglet and Rabbit and all of you. Don't you remember?"

"I do remember, and then when I try to remember, I forget."

"That day when Pooh and Piglet tried to catch the Heffalump —"

"They didn't catch it, did they?"

"No."

"Pooh couldn't, because he hasn't any brain. Did *I* catch it?"

"Well, that comes into the story."

Christopher Robin nodded.

"I do remember," he said, "only Pooh doesn't very well, so that's why he likes having it told to him again. Because then it's a real story and not just a remembering."

"That's just how *I* feel," I said.

Christopher Robin gave a deep sigh, picked his Bear up by the leg, and walked off to the door, trailing Pooh behind him. At the door he turned and said, "Coming to see me have my bath?"

"I might," I said.

"I didn't hurt him when I shot him, did I?"

"Not a bit."

He nodded and went out, and in a moment I heard Winnie-the-Pooh – *bump, bump, bump* – going up the stairs behind him.

HAPPINESS

John had
Great Big
Waterproof
Boots on;
John had a
Great Big
Waterproof
Hat;
John had a
Great Big
Waterproof
Mackintosh –
And that
(Said John)
    Is
      That.

Lines and Squares

Whenever I walk in a London street,
I'm ever so careful to watch my feet;
    And I keep in the squares,
    And the masses of bears,
Who wait at the corners all ready to eat
The sillies who tread on the lines of the street,
    Go back to their lairs,
    And I say to them, "Bears,
Just look how I'm walking in all the squares!"

And the little bears growl to each other, "He's mine,
As soon as he's silly and steps on a line."
And some of the bigger bears try to pretend
That they came round the corner to look for a friend;
And they try to pretend that nobody cares
Whether you walk on the lines or squares.
But only the sillies believe their talk;
It's ever so portant how you walk.
And it's ever so jolly to call out, "Bears,
Just watch me walking in all the squares!"

Pooh Goes Visiting and gets into a Tight Place

Edward Bear, known to his friends as Winnie-the-Pooh, or Pooh for short, was walking through the Forest one day, humming proudly to himself. He had made up a little hum that very morning, as he was doing his Stoutness Exercises in front of the glass: *Tra-la-la, tra-la-la*, as he stretched up as high as he could go, and then *Tra-la-la, tra-la – oh, help! – la*, as he tried to reach his toes. After breakfast he had said it over and over to himself until he had learnt it off by heart, and now he was humming it right through, properly. It went like this:

> *Tra-la-la, tra-la-la,*
> *Tra-la-la, tra-la-la,*
> *Rum-tum-tiddle-um-tum.*
> *Tiddle-iddle, tiddle-iddle,*
> *Tiddle-iddle, tiddle-iddle,*
> *Rum-tum-tum-tiddle-um.*

Well, he was humming this hum to himself, and walking gaily along, wondering what everybody else was doing, and what it felt like, being somebody else, when suddenly he came to a sandy bank, and in the bank was a large hole.

"Aha!" said Pooh. (*Rum-tum-tiddle-um-tum.*) "If I know anything about anything, that hole means Rabbit," he said, "and Rabbit means Company," he said, "and Company means Food and Listening-to-Me-Humming and such like. *Rum-tum-tum-tiddle-um.*"

So he bent down, put his head into the hole, and called out:

"Is anybody at home?"

There was a sudden scuffling noise from inside the hole, and then silence.

"What I said was, 'Is anybody at home?' " called out Pooh very loudly.

"No!" said a voice; and then added, "You needn't shout so loud. I heard you quite well the first time."

"Bother!" said Pooh. "Isn't there anybody here at all?"

"Nobody."

Winnie-the-Pooh took his head out of the hole, and thought for a little, and he thought to himself, "There must be somebody there, because somebody must have *said* 'Nobody'." So he put his head back in the hole, and said:

"Hallo, Rabbit, isn't that you?"

"No," said Rabbit, in a different sort of voice this time.

"But isn't that Rabbit's voice?"

"I don't *think* so," said Rabbit. "It isn't *meant* to be."

"Oh!" said Pooh.

He took his head out of the hole, and had another think, and then he put it back, and said:

"Well, could you very kindly tell me where Rabbit is?"

"He has gone to see his friend Pooh Bear, who is a great friend of his."

"But this *is* Me!" said Bear, very much surprised.

"What sort of Me?"

"Pooh Bear."

"Are you sure?" said Rabbit, still more surprised.

"Quite, quite sure," said Pooh.

"Oh, well, then, come in."

So Pooh pushed and pushed and pushed his way through the hole, and at last he got in.

"You were quite right," said Rabbit, looking at him all over. "It *is* you. Glad to see you."

"Who did you think it was?"

"Well, I wasn't sure. You know how it is in the Forest. One can't have *anybody* coming into one's house. One has to be *careful*. What about a mouthful of something?"

Pooh always liked a little something at eleven o'clock in the morning, and he was very glad to see Rabbit getting out the plates and mugs; and when Rabbit said, "Honey or condensed milk with your bread?" he was so excited that he said, "Both," and then, so as not to seem greedy, he added, "But don't bother about the bread, please." And for a long time after that he said nothing . . . until at last, humming to himself in a rather sticky voice, he got up, shook Rabbit lovingly by the paw, and said that he must be going on.

"Must you?" said Rabbit politely.

"Well," said Pooh, "I could stay a little longer if it – if you —" and he tried very hard to look in the direction of the larder.

"As a matter of fact," said Rabbit, "I was going out myself directly."

"Oh well, then, I'll be going on. Good-bye."

"Well, good-bye, if you're sure you won't have any more."

"*Is* there any more?" asked Pooh quickly.

Rabbit took the covers off the dishes, and said, "No, there wasn't."

"I thought not," said Pooh, nodding to himself. "Well, good-bye, I must be going on."

So he started to climb out of the hole. He pulled with his front paws, and pushed with his back paws, and in a little while his nose was out in the open again . . . and then his ears . . . and then his front paws . . . and then his shoulders . . . and then —

"Oh, help!" said Pooh. "I'd better go back."

"Oh, bother!" said Pooh. "I shall have to go on."

"I can't do either!" said Pooh. "Oh, help *and* bother!"

Now, by this time Rabbit wanted to go for a walk too, and finding the front door full, he went out by the back door, and came round to Pooh, and looked at him.

"Hallo, are you stuck?" he asked.

"N-no," said Pooh carelessly. "Just resting and thinking and humming to myself."

"Here, give us a paw."

Pooh Bear stretched out a paw, and Rabbit pulled and pulled and pulled. . . .

"*Ow!*" cried Pooh. "You're hurting!"

"The fact is," said Rabbit, "you're stuck."

"It all comes," said Pooh crossly, "of not having front doors big enough."

"It all comes," said Rabbit sternly, "of eating too much. I thought at the time," said Rabbit, "only I didn't like to say anything," said Rabbit, "that one of us was eating too much," said Rabbit, "and I knew it wasn't *me*," he said. "Well, well, I shall go and fetch Christopher Robin."

Christopher Robin lived at the other end of the Forest, and when he came back with Rabbit, and saw the front half of Pooh, he said, "Silly old Bear," in such a loving voice that everybody felt quite hopeful again.

"I was just beginning to think," said Bear, sniffing slightly, "that Rabbit might never be able to use his front door again. And I should *hate* that," he said.

"So should I," said Rabbit.

"Use his front door again?" said Christopher Robin. "Of course he'll use his front door again."

"Good," said Rabbit.

"If we can't pull you out, Pooh, we might push you back."

Rabbit scratched his whiskers thoughtfully, and pointed out that, when once Pooh was pushed back, he was back, and of course nobody was more glad to see Pooh than *he* was, still there it was, some lived in trees and some lived underground, and —

"You mean I'd *never* get out?" said Pooh.

"I mean," said Rabbit, "that having got *so* far, it seems a pity to waste it."

Christopher Robin nodded.

"Then there's only one thing to be done," he said. "We shall have to wait for you to get thin again."

"How long does getting thin take?"
asked Pooh anxiously.

"About a week, I should think."

"But I can't stay here for a *week*!"

"You can *stay* here all right, silly old Bear. It's getting you out which is so difficult."

"We'll read to you," said Rabbit cheerfully.

"And I hope it won't snow," he added. "And I say, old fellow, you're taking up a good deal of room in my house – *do* you mind if I use your back legs as a towel-horse? Because, I mean, there they are – doing nothing – and it would be very convenient just to hang the towels on them."

"A week!" said Pooh gloomily. "*What about meals?*"

"I'm afraid no meals," said Christopher Robin, "because of getting thin quicker. But we *will* read to you."

Bear began to sigh, and then found he couldn't because he was so tightly stuck; and a tear rolled down his eye, as he said:

"Then would you read a Sustaining Book, such as would help and comfort a Wedged Bear in Great Tightness?"

So for a week Christopher Robin read that sort of book at the North end of Pooh, and

Rabbit hung his washing on the South end . . . and in between Bear felt himself getting slenderer and slenderer. And at the end of the week Christopher Robin said, "*Now!*"

So he took hold of Pooh's front paws and Rabbit took hold of Christopher Robin, and all Rabbit's friends-and-relations took hold of Rabbit, and they all pulled together. . . .

And for a long time Pooh only said

"*Ow!*" . . .

And "*Oh!*" . . .

And then, all of a sudden, he said "*Pop!*" just as if a cork were coming out of a bottle.

And Christopher Robin and Rabbit and all Rabbit's friends-and-relations went head-over-heels backwards . . . and on the top of them came Winnie-the-Pooh – free!

So, with a nod of thanks to his friends, he went on with his walk through the forest, humming proudly to himself. But Christopher Robin looked after him lovingly, and said to himself, "Silly old Bear!"

TEDDY BEAR

A bear, however hard he tries,
Grows tubby without exercise.
Our Teddy Bear is short and fat,
Which is not to be wondered at;
He gets what exercise he can
By falling off the ottoman,
But generally seems to lack
The energy to clamber back.

Now tubbiness is just the thing
Which gets a fellow wondering;
And Teddy worried lots about
The fact that he was rather stout.
He thought: "If only I were thin!
But how does anyone begin?"
He thought: "It really isn't fair
To grudge me exercise and air."

For many weeks he pressed in vain
His nose against the window-pane,
And envied those who walked about
Reducing their unwanted stout.
None of the people he could see
"Is quite" (he said) "as fat as me!"
Then, with a still more moving sigh,
"I mean" (he said) "as fat as I!"

Now Teddy, as was only right,
Slept in the ottoman at night,
And with him crowded in as well
More animals than I can tell;
Not only these, but books and things,
Such as a kind relation brings –
Old tales of "Once upon a time,"
And history retold in rhyme.

One night it happened that he took
A peep at an old picture book,
Wherein he came across by chance
The picture of a King of France
(A stoutish man) and, down below,
These words: "King Louis So and So,
Nicknamed 'The Handsome'!" There he sat,
And (think of it!) the man was fat!

Our bear rejoiced like anything
To read about this famous King,
Nicknamed "The Handsome". There he sat,
And certainly the man was fat.
Nicknamed "The Handsome". Not a doubt
The man was definitely stout.
Why then, a bear (for all his tub)
Might yet be named "The Handsome Cub"!
"Might yet be named." Or did he mean

That years ago he "might have been"?
For now he felt a slight misgiving:
"Is Louis So and So still living?
Fashions in beauty have a way
Of altering from day to day.
Is 'Handsome Louis' with us yet?
Unfortunately I forget."
Next morning (nose to window-pane)

The doubt occurred to him again.
One question hammered in his head:
"Is he alive or is he dead?"
Thus, nose to pane, he pondered; but
The lattice window, loosely shut,
Swung open. With one startled "Oh!"
Our Teddy disappeared below.

There happened to be passing by
A plump man with a twinkling eye,
Who, seeing Teddy in the street,
Raised him politely to his feet,
And murmured kindly in his ear
Soft words of comfort and of cheer:
"Well, well!" "Allow me!" "Not at all."
"Tut-tut! A very nasty fall."
Our Teddy answered not a word;

Our Teddy answered not a word;
It's doubtful if he even heard.
Our bear could only look and look:
The stout man in the picture book!
That "handsome" King – could this be he,
This man of adiposity?
"Impossible," he thought. "But still,
No harm in asking. Yes I will!"

"Are you," he said, "by any chance
His Majesty the King of France?"
The other answered, "I am that,"
Bowed stiffly, and removed his hat;
Then said, "Excuse me," with an air,
"But is it Mr Edward Bear?"
And Teddy, bending very low,
Replied politely, "Even so!"

They stood beneath the window there,
The King and Mr Edward Bear,
And, handsome, if a trifle fat,
Talked carelessly of this and that . . .
Then said His Majesty, "Well, well,
I must get on," and rang the bell.
"Your bear, I think," he smiled. "Good-day!"
And turned, and went upon his way.

A bear, however hard he tries,
Grows tubby without exercise.
Our Teddy Bear is short and fat,
Which is not to be wondered at.
But do you think it worries him
To know that he is far from slim?
No, just the other way about –
He's *proud* of being short and stout.

Eeyore has a Birthday

Eeyore, the old grey Donkey, stood by the side of the stream, and looked at himself in the water.

"Pathetic," he said. "That's what it is. Pathetic."

He turned and walked slowly down the stream for twenty yards, splashed across it, and walked slowly back on the other side. Then he looked at himself in the water again.

"As I thought," he said. "No better from *this* side. But nobody minds. Nobody cares. Pathetic, that's what it is."

There was a crackling noise in the bracken behind him, and out came Pooh.

"Good morning, Eeyore," said Pooh.

"Good morning, Pooh Bear," said Eeyore gloomily. "If it *is* a good morning," he said. "Which I doubt," said he.

"Why, what's the matter?"

"Nothing, Pooh Bear, nothing. We can't all, and some of us don't. That's all there is to it."

"Can't all *what?*" said Pooh, rubbing his nose.

"Gaiety. Song-and-dance. Here we go round the mulberry bush."

"Oh!" said Pooh. He thought for a long time, and then asked, "What mulberry bush is that?"

"Bon-hommy," went on Eeyore gloomily. "French word meaning bonhommy," he explained. "I'm not complaining, but There It Is."

Pooh sat down on a large stone, and tried to think this out. It sounded to him like a riddle, and he was never much good at riddles, being a Bear of Very Little Brain. So he sang *Cottleston Pie* instead:

> Cottleston, Cottleston, Cottleston Pie,
> A fly can't bird, but a bird can fly.
> Ask me a riddle and I reply:
> *"Cottleston, Cottleston, Cottleston Pie."*

That was the first verse. When he had finished it, Eeyore didn't actually say that he didn't like it, so Pooh very kindly sang the second verse to him:

> Cottleston, Cottleston, Cottleston Pie,
> A fish can't whistle and neither can I.
> Ask me a riddle and I reply:
> *"Cottleston, Cottleston, Cottleston Pie."*

Eeyore still said nothing at all, so Pooh hummed the third verse quietly to himself:

> Cottleston, Cottleston, Cottleston Pie,
> Why does a chicken, I don't know why.
> Ask me a riddle and I reply:
> *"Cottleston, Cottleston, Cottleston Pie."*

"That's right," said Eeyore. "Sing. Umty-tiddly, umpty-too. Here we go gathering Nuts and May. Enjoy yourself."

"I am," said Pooh.

"Some can," said Eeyore.

"Why, what's the matter?"

"*Is* anything the matter?"

"You seem so sad, Eeyore."

"Sad? Why should I be sad? It's my birthday. The happiest day of the year."

"Your birthday?" said Pooh in great surprise.

"Of course it is. Can't you see? Look at all the presents I have had."

He waved a foot from side to side.
"Look at the birthday cake. Candles
and pink sugar."

Pooh looked – first to the right and
then to the left.

"Presents?" said Pooh. "Birthday
cake?" said Pooh. "*Where?*"

"Can't you see them?"

"No," said Pooh.

"Neither can I," said Eeyore. "Joke," he explained. "Ha ha!"

Pooh scratched his head, being a little puzzled by all this.

"But is it really your birthday?" he asked.

"It is."

"Oh! Well, many happy returns of the day, Eeyore."

"And many happy returns to you, Pooh Bear."

"But it isn't *my* birthday."

"No, it's mine."

"But you said 'Many happy returns' —"

"Well, why not? You don't always want to be miserable on my birthday,
do you?"

"Oh, I see," said Pooh.

"It's bad enough," said Eeyore, almost breaking down, "being miserable
myself, what with no presents and no cake and no candles, and no proper
notice taken of me at all, but if everybody else is going to be miserable too —"

This was too much for Pooh. "Stay there!" he called to Eeyore, as he
turned and hurried back home as quick as he could; for he felt that he must
get poor Eeyore a present of *some* sort at once, and he could always think of
a proper one afterwards.

Outside his house he found Piglet, jumping up and down trying to reach
the knocker.

"Hallo, Piglet," he said.

"Hallo, Pooh," said Piglet.

"What are *you* trying to do?"

"I was trying to reach the knocker," said Piglet. "I just came round —"

"Let me do it for you," said Pooh kindly. So he reached up and knocked at the door. "I have just seen Eeyore," he began, "and poor Eeyore is in a Very Sad Condition, because it's his birthday, and nobody has taken any notice of it, and he's very Gloomy – you know what Eeyore is – and there he was, and — What a long time whoever lives here is answering this door." And he knocked again.

"But, Pooh," said Piglet, "it's your own house!"

"Oh!" said Pooh. "So it is," he said. "Well, let's go in."

So in they went. The first thing Pooh did was to go to the cupboard to see if he had quite a small jar of honey left; and he had, so he took it down.

"I'm giving this to Eeyore," he explained, "as a present. What are *you* going to give?"

"Couldn't I give it too?" said Piglet. "From both of us?"

"No," said Pooh. "That would *not* be a good plan."

"All right, then, I'll give him a balloon. I've got one left from my party. I'll go and get it now, shall I?"

"That, Piglet, is a *very* good idea. It is just what Eeyore wants to cheer him up. Nobody can be uncheered with a balloon."

So off Piglet trotted; and in the other direction went Pooh, with his jar of honey.

It was a warm day, and he had a long way to go. He hadn't gone more than half-way when a sort of funny feeling began to creep all over him. It began at the tip of his nose and trickled all through him and out at the soles of his feet. It was just as if somebody inside him were saying, "Now then, Pooh, time for a little something."

"Dear, dear," said Pooh, "I didn't know it was as late as that." So he sat down and took the top off his jar of honey. "Lucky I brought this with me," he thought. "Many a bear going out on a warm day like this would never have thought of bringing a little something with him." And he began to eat.

"Now let me see," he thought, as he took his last lick of the inside of the jar, "where was I going? Ah, yes, Eeyore." He got up slowly.

And then, suddenly, he remembered. He had eaten Eeyore's birthday present!

"*Bother!*" said Pooh. "What *shall* I do? I *must* give him *something*."

For a little while he couldn't think of anything. Then he thought: "Well, it's a very nice pot, even if there's no honey in it, and if I washed it clean, and got somebody to write 'A *Happy Birthday*' on it, Eeyore could keep things in it, which might be Useful." So, as he was just passing the Hundred Acre Wood, he went inside to call on Owl, who lived there.

"Good morning, Owl," he said.

"Good morning, Pooh," said Owl.

"Many happy returns of Eeyore's birthday," said Pooh.

"Oh, is that what it is?"

"What are you giving him, Owl?"

"What are *you* giving him, Pooh?"

"I'm giving him a Useful Pot to Keep Things In, and I wanted to ask you —"

"Is this it?" said Owl, taking it out of Pooh's paw.

"Yes, and I wanted to ask you —"

"Somebody has been keeping honey in it," said Owl.

"You can keep *anything* in it," said Pooh earnestly. "It's Very Useful like that. And I wanted to ask you —"

"You ought to write 'A *Happy Birthday*' on it."

"*That* was what I wanted to ask you," said Pooh. "Because my spelling is Wobbly. It's good spelling but it Wobbles, and the letters get in the wrong places. Would *you* write 'A Happy Birthday' on it for me?"

"It's a nice pot," said Owl, looking at it all round. "Couldn't I give it too? From both of us?"

"No," said Pooh. "That would *not* be a good plan. Now I'll just wash it first, and then you can write on it."

Well, he washed the pot out, and dried it, while Owl licked the end of his pencil, and wondered how to spell "birthday".

"Can you read, Pooh?" he asked a little anxiously. "There's a notice about knocking and ringing outside my door, which Christopher Robin wrote. Could you read it?"

"Christopher Robin told me what it said, and *then* I could."

"Well, I'll tell you what *this* says, and then you'll be able to."

So Owl wrote . . . and this is what he wrote:

HIPY PAPY BTHUTHDTH THUTHDA BTHUTHDY.

Pooh looked on admiringly.

"I'm just saying 'A Happy Birthday'," said Owl carelessly.

"It's a nice long one," said Pooh, very much impressed by it.

"Well, *actually*, of course, I'm saying 'A Very Happy Birthday with love from Pooh.' Naturally it takes a good deal of pencil to say a long thing like that."

"Oh, I see," said Pooh.

While all this was happening, Piglet had gone back to his own house to get Eeyore's balloon. He held it very tightly against himself, so that it shouldn't blow away, and he ran as fast as he could so as to get to Eeyore before Pooh did; for he thought that he would like to be the first one to give a present, just as if he had thought of it without being told by anybody. And running along, and thinking how pleased Eeyore would be, he didn't look where he was going . . . and suddenly he put his foot in a rabbit hole, and fell down flat on his face.

BANG!!!???***!!!

Piglet lay there, wondering what had happened. At first he thought that the whole world had blown up; and then he thought that perhaps only the Forest part of it had; and then he thought that perhaps only *he* had, and he was now alone in the moon or somewhere, and would never see Christopher Robin or Pooh or Eeyore again. And then he thought, "Well, even if I'm in the moon, I needn't be face downwards all the time," so he got cautiously up and looked about him.

He was still in the Forest!

"Well, that's funny," he thought. "I wonder what that bang was. I couldn't have made such a noise just falling down. And where's my balloon? And what's that small piece of damp rag doing?"

It was the balloon!

"Oh, dear!" said Piglet. "Oh, dear, oh, dearie, dearie, dear! Well, it's too late now. I can't go back, and I haven't another balloon, and perhaps Eeyore doesn't *like* balloons so *very* much."

So he trotted on, rather sadly now, and down he came to the side of the stream where Eeyore was, and called out to him.

"Good morning, Eeyore," shouted Piglet.

"Good morning, Little Piglet," said Eeyore. "If it *is* a good morning," he said. "Which I doubt," said he. "Not that it matters," he said.

"Many happy returns of the day," said Piglet, having now got closer.

Eeyore stopped looking at himself in the stream, and turned to stare at Piglet.

"Just say that again," he said.

"Many hap —"

"Wait a moment."

Balancing on three legs, he began to bring his fourth leg very cautiously up to his ear. "I did this yesterday," he explained, as he fell down for the third time. "It's quite easy. It's so as I can hear better. . . . There, that's done it! Now then, what were you saying?" He pushed his ear forward with his hoof.

"Many happy returns of the day," said Piglet again.

"Meaning me?"

"Of course, Eeyore."

"My birthday?"

"Yes."

"Me having a real birthday?"

"Yes, Eeyore, and I've brought you a present."

Eeyore took down his right hoof from his right ear, turned round, and with great difficulty put up his left hoof.

"I must have that in the other ear," he said. "Now then."

"A present," said Piglet very loudly.

"Meaning me again?"

"Yes."

"My birthday still?"

"Of course, Eeyore."

"Me going on having a real birthday?"

"Yes, Eeyore, and I brought you a balloon."

"*Balloon?*" said Eeyore. "You did say balloon? One of those big coloured things you blow up? Gaiety, song-and-dance, here we are and there we are?"

"Yes, but I'm afraid – I'm very sorry, Eeyore – but when I was running along to bring it you, I fell down."

"Dear, dear, how unlucky! You ran too fast, I expect. You didn't hurt yourself, Little Piglet?"

"No, but I – I – oh, Eeyore, I burst the balloon!"

There was a very long silence.

"My balloon?" said Eeyore at last.

Piglet nodded.

"My birthday balloon?"

"Yes, Eeyore," said Piglet, sniffing a little. "Here it is. With – with many happy returns of the day." And he gave Eeyore the small piece of damp rag.

"Is this it?" said Eeyore, a little surprised.

Piglet nodded.

"My present?"

Piglet nodded again.

"The balloon?"

"Yes."

"Thank you, Piglet," said Eeyore. "You don't mind my asking," he went on, "but what colour was this balloon when it – when it *was* a balloon?"

"Red."

"I just wondered. . . . Red," he murmured to himself. "My favourite colour. . . . How big was it?"

"About as big as me."

"I just wondered. . . . About as big as Piglet," he said to himself sadly. "My favourite size. Well, well."

Piglet felt very miserable, and didn't know what to say. He was still opening his mouth to begin something, and then deciding that it wasn't any good saying *that*, when he heard a shout from the other side of the river, and there was Pooh.

"Many happy returns of the day," called out Pooh, forgetting that he had said it already.

"Thank you, Pooh, I'm having them," said Eeyore gloomily.

"I've brought you a little present," said Pooh excitedly.

"I've had it," said Eeyore.

Pooh had now splashed across the stream to Eeyore, and Piglet was sitting a little way off, his head in his paws, snuffling to himself.

"It's a Useful Pot," said Pooh. "Here it is. And it's got 'A Very Happy Birthday with love from Pooh' written on it. That's what all that writing is. And it's for putting things in. There!"

When Eeyore saw the pot, he became quite excited. "Why!" he said. "I believe my Balloon will just go into that Pot!"

"Oh, no, Eeyore," said Pooh. "Balloons are much too big to go into Pots. What you do with a balloon is, you hold the balloon —"

"Not mine," said Eeyore proudly. "Look, Piglet!" And as Piglet looked sorrowfully round, Eeyore picked the balloon up with his teeth, and placed it carefully in the pot; picked it out and put it on the ground; and then picked it up again and put it carefully back.

"So it does!" said Pooh. "It goes in!"

"So it does!" said Piglet. "And it comes out!"

"Doesn't it?" said Eeyore. "It goes in and out like anything."

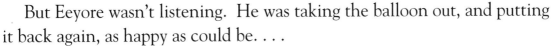

"I'm very glad," said Pooh happily, "that I thought of giving you a Useful Pot to put things in."

"I'm very glad," said Piglet happily, "that I thought of giving you Something to put in a Useful Pot."

But Eeyore wasn't listening. He was taking the balloon out, and putting it back again, as happy as could be. . . .

"And didn't *I* give him anything?" asked Christopher Robin sadly.

"Of course you did," I said. "You gave him – don't you remember – a little – a little —"

"I gave him a box of paints to paint things with."

"That was it."

"Why didn't I give it to him in the morning?"

"You were so busy getting his party ready for him. He had a cake with icing on the top, and three candles, and his name in pink sugar, and —"

"Yes, *I* remember," said Christopher Robin.

BUCKINGHAM PALACE

They're changing guard at Buckingham Palace –
Christopher Robin went down with Alice.
Alice is marrying one of the guard.
"A soldier's life is terrible hard,"
                                        Says Alice.

They're changing guard at Buckingham Palace –
Christopher Robin went down with Alice.
We saw a guard in a sentry-box.
"One of the sergeants looks after their socks,"
                                        Says Alice.

They're changing guard at Buckingham Palace –
Christopher Robin went down with Alice.
We looked for the King, but he never came.
"Well, God take care of him, all the same,"
                                        Says Alice.

They're changing guard at Buckingham Palace –
Christopher Robin went down with Alice.
They've great big parties inside the grounds.
"I wouldn't be King for a hundred pounds,"
       Says Alice.

They're changing guard at Buckingham Palace –
Christopher Robin went down with Alice.
A face looked out, but it wasn't the King's.
"He's much too busy a-signing things,"
       Says Alice.

They're changing guard at Buckingham Palace –
Christopher Robin went down with Alice.
"Do you think the King knows all about *me*?"
"Sure to, dear, but it's time for tea,"
       Says Alice.

Kanga and Baby Roo Come to the Forest

Nobody seemed to know where they came from, but there they were in the Forest: Kanga and Baby Roo. When Pooh asked Christopher Robin, "How did they come here?" Christopher Robin said, "In the Usual Way, if you know what I mean, Pooh," and Pooh, who didn't, said "Oh!" Then he nodded his head twice and said, "In the Usual Way. Ah!" Then he went to call upon his friend Piglet to see what *he* thought about it. And at Piglet's house he found Rabbit. So they all talked about it together.

"What I don't like about it is this," said Rabbit. "Here are we – you, Pooh, and you, Piglet, and Me – and suddenly —"

"And Eeyore," said Pooh.

"And Eeyore – and then suddenly —"

"And Owl," said Pooh.

"And Owl – and then all of a sudden —"

"Oh, and Eeyore," said Pooh. "I was forgetting *him*."

"Here – we – are," said Rabbit very slowly and carefully, "all – of – us, and then, suddenly, we wake up one morning, and what do we find? We find a Strange Animal among us. An animal of whom we had never even heard before! An animal who carries her family about with her in her pocket! Suppose *I* carried *my* family about with me in *my* pocket, how many pockets should I want?"

"Sixteen," said Piglet.

"Seventeen, isn't it?" said Rabbit. "And one more for a handkerchief – that's eighteen. Eighteen pockets in one suit! I haven't time."

There was a long and thoughtful silence . . . and then Pooh, who had been frowning very hard for some minutes, said: "*I* make it fifteen."

"What?" said Rabbit.

"Fifteen."

"Fifteen what?"

"Your family."

"What about them?"

Pooh rubbed his nose and said that he thought Rabbit had been talking about his family.

"Did I?" said Rabbit carelessly.

"Yes, you said —"

"Never mind, Pooh," said Piglet impatiently. "The question is, What are we to do about Kanga?"

"Oh, I see," said Pooh.

"The best way," said Rabbit, "would be this. The best way would be to steal Baby Roo and hide him, and then when Kanga says, 'Where's Baby Roo?' we say, '*Aha!*' "

"*Aha!*" said Pooh, practising. "*Aha! Aha!* . . . Of course," he went on, "we could say '*Aha!*' even if we hadn't stolen Baby Roo."

"Pooh," said Rabbit kindly, "you haven't any brain."

"I know," said Pooh humbly.

"We say '*Aha!*' so that Kanga knows that *we* know where Baby Roo is. '*Aha!*' means 'We'll tell you where Baby Roo is, if you promise to go away from the Forest and never come back.' Now don't talk while I think."

Pooh went into a corner and tried saying '*Aha!*' in that sort of voice. Sometimes it seemed to him that it did mean what Rabbit said, and sometimes it seemed to him that it didn't. "I suppose it's just practice," he thought. " I wonder if Kanga will have to practise too so as to understand it."

"There's just one thing," said Piglet, fidgeting a bit. "I was talking to Christopher Robin, and he said that a Kanga was Generally Regarded as One of the Fiercer Animals. I am not frightened of Fierce Animals in the ordinary way, but it is well known that if One of the Fiercer Animals is Deprived of Its Young, it becomes as fierce as Two of the Fiercer Animals. In which case '*Aha!*' is perhaps a *foolish* thing to say."

"Piglet," said Rabbit, taking out a pencil, and licking the end of it, "you haven't any pluck."

"It is hard to be brave," said Piglet, sniffing slightly, "when you're only a Very Small Animal."

Rabbit, who had begun to write very busily, looked up and said:

"It is because you are a very small animal that you will be Useful in the adventure before us."

Piglet was so excited at the idea of being Useful that he forgot to be frightened any more, and when Rabbit went on to say that Kangas were only Fierce during the winter months, being at other times of an Affectionate Disposition, he could hardly sit still, he was so eager to begin being useful at once.

"What about me?" said Pooh sadly. "I suppose *I* shan't be useful?"

"Never mind, Pooh," said Piglet comfortingly. "Another time perhaps."

"Without Pooh," said Rabbit solemnly as he sharpened his pencil, "the adventure would be impossible."

"Oh!" said Piglet, and tried not to look disappointed. But Pooh went into a corner of the room and said proudly to himself, "Impossible without Me! *That* sort of Bear."

"Now listen all of you," said Rabbit when he had finished writing, and Pooh and Piglet sat listening very eagerly with their mouths open. This was what Rabbit read out:

PLAN TO CAPTURE BABY ROO

1. *General Remarks.* Kanga runs faster than any of Us, even Me.
2. *More General Remarks.* Kanga never takes her eye off Baby Roo, except when he's safely buttoned up in her pocket.
3. *Therefore.* If we are to capture Baby Roo, we must get a Long Start, because Kanga runs faster than any of Us, even Me. (*See* 1.)
4. *A Thought.* If Roo had jumped out of Kanga's pocket and Piglet had jumped in, Kanga wouldn't know the difference, because Piglet is a Very Small Animal.
5. Like Roo.

6. But Kanga would have to be looking the other way first, so as not to see Piglet jumping in.

7. See 2.

8. *Another Thought.* But if Pooh was talking to her very excitedly, she *might* look the other way for a moment.

9. And then I could run away with Roo.

10. Quickly.

11. *And Kanga wouldn't discover the difference until Afterwards.*

Well, Rabbit read this out proudly, and for a little while after he had read it nobody said anything. And then Piglet, who had been opening and shutting his mouth without making any noise, managed to say very huskily:

"And – Afterwards?"

"How do you mean?"

"When Kanga *does* Discover the Difference?"

"Then we all say 'Aha!'"

"All three of us?"

"Yes."

"Oh!"

"Why, what's the trouble, Piglet?"

"Nothing," said Piglet, "as long as *we all three* say it. As long as we all three say it," said Piglet, "I don't mind," he said, "but I shouldn't care to say 'Aha!' by myself. It wouldn't sound *nearly* so well. By the way," he said, "you *are* quite sure about what you said about the winter months?"

"The winter months?"

"Yes, only being Fierce in the Winter Months."

"Oh, yes, yes, that's all right. Well, Pooh? You see what you have to do?"

"No," said Pooh Bear. "Not yet," he said. "What *do* I do?"

"Well, you just have to talk very hard to Kanga so as she doesn't notice anything."

"Oh! What about?"

"Anything you like."

"You mean like telling her a little bit of poetry or something?"

"That's it," said Rabbit. "Splendid. Now come along."

So they all went out to look for Kanga.

Kanga and Roo were spending a quiet afternoon in a sandy part of the

Forest. Baby Roo was practising very small jumps in the sand, and falling down mouse-holes and climbing out of them, and Kanga was fidgeting about and saying "Just one more jump, dear, and then we must go home." And at that moment who should come stumping up the hill but Pooh.

"Good afternoon, Kanga."

"Good afternoon, Pooh."

"Look at me jumping," squeaked Roo, and fell into another mouse-hole.

"Hallo, Roo, my little fellow!"

"We were just going home," said Kanga. "Good afternoon, Rabbit. Good afternoon, Piglet."

Rabbit and Piglet, who had now come up from the other side of the hill, said "Good afternoon," and "Hallo, Roo," and Roo asked them to look at him jumping, so they stayed and looked.

And Kanga looked too. . . .

"Oh, Kanga," said Pooh, after Rabbit had winked at him twice, "I don't know if you are interested in Poetry at all?"

"Hardly at all," said Kanga.

"Oh!" said Pooh.

"Roo, dear, just one more jump and then we must go home."

There was a short silence while Roo fell down another mouse-hole.

"Go on," said Rabbit in a loud whisper behind his paw.

"Talking of Poetry," said Pooh, "I made up a little piece as I was coming along. It went like this. Er – now let me see —"

"Fancy!" said Kanga. "Now, Roo, dear —"

"You'll like this piece of poetry," said Rabbit.

"You'll love it," said Piglet.

"You must listen very carefully," said Rabbit.

"So as not to miss any of it," said Piglet.

"Oh, yes," said Kanga, but she still looked at Baby Roo.

"*How* did it go, Pooh?" said Rabbit.

Pooh gave a little cough and began.

LINES WRITTEN BY A BEAR
OF VERY LITTLE BRAIN

On Monday, when the sun is hot
I wonder to myself a lot:
"Now is it true, or is it not,
"That what is which and which is what?"

On Tuesday, when it hails and snows,
The feeling on me grows and grows
That hardly anybody knows
If those are these or these are those.

On Wednesday, when the sky is blue,
And I have nothing else to do,
I sometimes wonder if it's true
That who is what and what is who.

On Thursday, when it starts to freeze
And hoar-frost twinkles on the trees,
How very readily one sees
That these are whose – but whose are these?

On Friday —

"Yes, it is, isn't it?" said Kanga, not waiting to hear what happened on Friday. "Just one more jump, Roo, dear, and then we really *must* be going."

Rabbit gave Pooh a hurrying-up sort of nudge.

"Talking of Poetry," said Pooh quickly, "have you ever noticed that tree right over there?"

"Where?" said Kanga. "Now, Roo —"

"Right over there," said Pooh, pointing behind Kanga's back.

"No," said Kanga. "Now jump in, Roo, dear, and we'll go home."

"You ought to look at that tree right over there," said Rabbit. "Shall I lift you in, Roo?" And he picked up Roo in his paws.

"I can see a bird in it from here," said Pooh. "Or is it a fish?"

"You ought to see that bird from here," said Rabbit. "Unless it's a fish."

"It isn't a fish, it's a bird," said Piglet.

"So it is," said Rabbit.

"Is it a starling or a blackbird?" said Pooh.

"That's the whole question," said Rabbit. "Is it a blackbird or a starling?"

And then at last Kanga did turn her head to look. And the moment that her head was turned, Rabbit said in a loud voice "In you go, Roo!" and in jumped Piglet into Kanga's pocket, and off scampered Rabbit, with Roo in his paws, as fast as he could.

"Why, where's Rabbit?" said Kanga, turning round again. "Are you all right, Roo, dear?"

Piglet made a squeaky Roo-noise from the bottom of Kanga's pocket.

"Rabbit had to go away," said Pooh. "I think he thought of something he

had to go and see about suddenly."

"And Piglet?"

"I think Piglet thought of something at the same time. Suddenly."

"Well, we must be getting home," said Kanga. "Good-bye, Pooh." And in three large jumps she was gone.

Pooh looked after her as she went.

"I wish I could jump like that," he thought. "Some can and some can't. That's how it is."

But there were moments when Piglet wished that Kanga couldn't. Often, when he had had a long walk home through the Forest, he had wished that he were a bird; but now he thought jerkily to himself at the bottom of Kanga's pocket,

"If this is flying I shall never really take to it."

And as he went up in the air he said, "Oooooo!" and as he came down he said, "Ow!" And he was saying, "Ooooooo-ow, Ooooooo-ow, Ooooooo-ow" all the way to Kanga's house.

Of course as soon as Kanga unbuttoned her pocket, she saw what had happened. Just for a moment, she thought she was frightened, and then she knew she wasn't; for she felt sure that Christopher Robin would never let any harm happen to Roo. So she said to herself, "If they are having a joke with me, I will have a joke with them."

"Now then, Roo, dear," she said, as she took Piglet out of her pocket, "Bed-time."

"*Aha!*" said Piglet, as well as he could after his Terrifying Journey. But it wasn't a very good "*Aha!*" and Kanga didn't seem to understand what it meant.

"Bath first," said Kanga in a cheerful voice.

"*Aha!*" said Piglet again, looking round anxiously for the others. But the others weren't there. Rabbit was playing with Baby Roo in his own house, and feeling more fond of him every minute, and Pooh, who had decided to be a Kanga, was still at the sandy place on the top of the Forest, practising jumps.

"I am not at all sure," said Kanga in a thoughtful voice, "that it wouldn't be a good idea to have a *cold* bath this evening. Would you like that, Roo, dear?"

Piglet, who had never been really fond of baths, shuddered a long indignant shudder, and said in as brave a voice as he could:

"Kanga, I see that the time has come to spleak painly."

"Funny little Roo," said Kanga, as she got the bath-water ready.

"I am *not* Roo," said Piglet loudly. "I am Piglet!"

"Yes, dear, yes," said Kanga soothingly. "And imitating Piglet's voice too! So clever of him," she went on, as she took a large bar of yellow soap out of the cupboard. "What *will* he be doing next?"

"Can't you *see*?" shouted Piglet. "Haven't you got *eyes*? *Look* at me!"

"I *am* looking, Roo, dear," said Kanga rather severely. "And you know what I told you yesterday about making faces. If you go on making faces like Piglet's, you will grow up to *look* like Piglet – and *then* think how sorry you will be. Now then, into the bath, and don't let me have to speak to you about it again."

Before he knew where he was, Piglet was in the bath, and Kanga was scrubbing him firmly with a large lathery flannel.

"*Ow!*" cried Piglet. "Let me out! I'm Piglet!"

"Don't open the mouth, dear, or the soap goes in," said Kanga. "There! What did I tell you?"

"You – you – you did it on purpose," spluttered Piglet, as soon as he could speak again . . . and then accidentally had another mouthful of lathery flannel.

"That's right, dear, don't say anything," said Kanga, and in another minute Piglet was out of the bath, and being rubbed dry with a towel.

"Now," said Kanga, "there's your medicine, and then bed."

"W-w-what medicine?" said Piglet.

"To make you grow big and strong, dear. You don't want to grow up small and weak like Piglet, do you? Well, then!"

At that moment there was a knock at the door.

"Come in," said Kanga, and in came Christopher Robin.

"Christopher Robin, Christopher Robin!" cried Piglet. "Tell Kanga who I am! She keeps saying I'm Roo. I'm *not* Roo, am I?"

Christopher Robin looked at him very carefully, and shook his head.

"You can't be Roo," he said, "because I've just seen Roo playing in Rabbit's house."

"Well!" said Kanga. "Fancy that! Fancy my making a mistake like that."

"There you are!" said Piglet. "I told you so. I'm Piglet."

Christopher Robin shook his head again.

"Oh, you're not Piglet," he said. "I know Piglet well, and he's *quite* a different colour."

Piglet began to say that this was because he had just had a bath, and then he thought that perhaps he wouldn't say that, and as he opened his mouth to say something else, Kanga slipped the medicine spoon in, and then patted him on the back and told him that it was really quite a nice taste when you got used to it.

"I knew it wasn't Piglet," said Kanga. "I wonder who it can be."

"Perhaps it's some relation of Pooh's," said Christopher Robin. "What about a nephew or an uncle or something?"

Kanga agreed that this was probably what it was, and said that they would have to call it by some name.

"I shall call it Pootel," said Christopher Robin. "Henry Pootel for short."

And just when it was decided, Henry Pootel wriggled out of Kanga's arms and jumped to the ground. To his great joy Christopher Robin had left the door open. Never had Henry Pootel Piglet run so fast as he ran then, and he didn't stop running until he had got quite close to his house. But when he was a hundred yards away he stopped running, and rolled the rest of the way home, so as to get his own nice comfortable colour again. . . .

So Kanga and Roo stayed in the Forest. And every Tuesday Roo spent the day with his great friend Rabbit, and every Tuesday Kanga spent the day with her great friend Pooh, teaching him to jump, and every Tuesday Piglet spent the day with his great friend Christopher Robin. So they were all happy again.

HOPPITY

Christopher Robin goes
Hoppity, hoppity,

Hoppity, hoppity, hop.
Whenever I tell him
Politely to stop it, he
Says he can't possibly stop.

If he stopped hopping, he
      couldn't go anywhere,
Poor little Christopher
Couldn't go anywhere . . .
That's why he *always* goes
Hoppity, hoppity,
Hoppity,
Hoppity,
Hop.

A THOUGHT

If I were John and John were Me,
Then he'd be six and I'd be three.
If John were Me and I were John,
I shouldn't have these trousers on.

Piglet is Entirely Surrounded by Water

It rained and it rained and it rained. Piglet told himself that never in all his life, and *he* was goodness knows *how* old – three, was it, or four? – never had he seen so much rain. Days and days and days.

"If only," he thought, as he looked out of the window, "I had been in Pooh's house, or Christopher Robin's house, or Rabbit's house when it began to rain, then I should have had Company all this time, instead of being here all alone, with nothing to do except wonder when it will stop." And he imagined himself with Pooh, saying, "Did you ever see such rain, Pooh?" and Pooh saying, "Isn't it *awful*, Piglet?" and Piglet saying, "I wonder how it is over Christopher Robin's way," and Pooh saying, "I should think poor old Rabbit is about flooded out by this time." It would have been jolly to talk like this, and really, it wasn't much good having anything exciting like floods, if you couldn't share them with somebody.

For it was rather exciting. The little dry ditches in which Piglet had nosed about so often had become streams, the little streams across which he had splashed were rivers, and the river, between whose steep banks they had played so happily, had sprawled out of its own bed and was taking up so much room everywhere, that Piglet was beginning to wonder whether it would be coming into *his* bed soon.

"It's a little Anxious," he said to himself, "to be a Very Small Animal Entirely Surrounded by Water. Christopher Robin and Pooh could escape by Climbing Trees, and Kanga could escape by Jumping, and Rabbit could escape by Burrowing, and Owl could escape by Flying, and Eeyore could escape by – by Making a Loud Noise Until Rescued, and here am I, surrounded by water and I can't do *anything*."

It went on raining, and every day the water got a little higher, until now it was nearly up to Piglet's window . . . and still he hadn't done anything.

"There's Pooh," he thought to himself. "Pooh hasn't much Brain, but he never comes to any harm. He does silly things and they turn out right. There's Owl. Owl hasn't exactly got Brain, but he Knows Things. He would know the Right Thing to Do when Surrounded by Water. There's Rabbit. He hasn't Learnt in Books, but he can always Think of a Clever Plan. There's Kanga. She isn't Clever, Kanga isn't, but she would be so anxious about Roo that she would do a Good Thing to Do without thinking about it. And then there's Eeyore. And Eeyore is so miserable anyhow that he wouldn't mind about this. But I wonder what Christopher Robin would do?"

Then suddenly he remembered a story which Christopher Robin had told him about a man on a desert island who had written something in a bottle and thrown it into the sea; and Piglet thought that if he wrote something in a bottle and threw it in the water, perhaps somebody would come and rescue *him*!

He left the window and began to search his house, all of it that wasn't under water, and at last he found a pencil and a small piece of dry paper, and a bottle with a cork to it. And he wrote on one side of the paper:

HELP!
PIGLIT (ME)

and on the other side:

IT'S ME PIGLIT, HELP HELP!

Then he put the paper in the bottle, and he corked the bottle up as tightly as he could, and he leant out of his window as far as he could lean without falling in, and he threw the bottle as far as he could throw – *splash!* – and in a little while it bobbed up again on the water; and he watched it floating slowly away in the distance, until his eyes ached with looking, and sometimes he thought it was the bottle, and sometimes he thought it was just a ripple on the water which he was following, and then suddenly he knew that he would never see it again and that he had done all that he could do to save himself.

"So now," he thought, "somebody else will have to do something, and I hope they will do it soon, because if they don't I shall have to swim, which I can't, so I hope they do it soon." And then he gave a very long sigh and said, "I wish Pooh were here. It's so much more friendly with two."

When the rain began Pooh was asleep. It rained, and it rained, and it rained, and he slept and he slept and he slept. He had had a tiring day. You remember how he discovered the North Pole; well, he was so proud of this that he asked Christopher Robin if there were any other Poles such as a Bear of Little Brain might discover.

"There's a South Pole," said Christopher Robin, "and I expect there's an East Pole and a West Pole, though people don't like talking about them."

Pooh was very excited when he heard this, and suggested that they should have an Expotition to discover the East Pole, but Christopher Robin had thought of something else to do with Kanga; so Pooh went out to discover the East Pole by himself. Whether he discovered it or not, I forget; but he was so tired when he got home that, in the very middle of his supper, after he had been eating for little more than half-an-hour, he fell fast asleep in his chair, and slept and slept and slept.

Then suddenly he was dreaming. He was at the East Pole, and it was a very cold pole with the coldest sort of snow and ice all over it. He had found a beehive to sleep in, but there wasn't room for his legs, so he had left them outside. And Wild Woozles, such as inhabit the East Pole, came and nibbled all the fur off his legs to make Nests for their Young. And the more they nibbled, the colder his legs got, until suddenly he woke up with an *Ow!* – and there he was, sitting in his chair with his feet in the water, and water all round him!

He splashed to his door and looked out. . . .

"This is Serious," said Pooh. "I must have an Escape."

So he took his largest pot of honey and escaped with it to a broad branch of his tree, well above the water, and then he climbed down again and escaped with another pot . . . and when the whole Escape was finished, there was Pooh sitting on his branch, dangling his legs, and there, beside him, were ten pots of honey. . . .

Two days later, there was Pooh, sitting on his branch, dangling his legs, and there, beside him, were four pots of honey. . . .

Three days later, there was Pooh, sitting on his branch, dangling his legs, and there, beside him, was one pot of honey.

Four days later, there was Pooh . . .

And it was on the morning of the fourth day that Piglet's bottle came floating past him, and with one loud cry of "Honey!" Pooh plunged into the water, seized the bottle, and struggled back to his tree again.

"Bother!" said Pooh, as he opened it. "All that wet for nothing. What's that bit of paper doing?"

He took it out and looked at it.

"It's a Missage," he said to himself, "that's what it is. And that letter is a 'P', and so is that, and so is that, and 'P' means 'Pooh', so it's a very important Missage to me, and I can't read it. I must find Christopher Robin or Owl or

Piglet, one of those Clever Readers who can read things, and they will tell me what this missage means. Only I can't swim. Bother!"

Then he had an idea, and I think that for a Bear of Very Little Brain, it was a good idea. He said to himself:

"If a bottle can float, then a jar can float, and if a jar floats, I can sit on the top of it, if it's a very big jar."

So he took his biggest jar, and corked it up.

"All boats have to have a name," he said, "so I shall call mine *The Floating Bear*." And with these words he dropped his boat into the water and jumped in after it.

For a little while Pooh and *The Floating Bear* were uncertain as to which of them was meant to be on the top, but after trying one or two different positions, they settled down with *The Floating Bear* underneath and Pooh triumphantly astride it, paddling vigorously with his feet.

Christopher Robin lived at the very top of the Forest. It rained, and it rained, and it rained, but the water couldn't come up to *his* house. It was rather jolly to look down into the valleys and see the water all round him, but it rained so hard that he stayed indoors most of the time, and thought about things. Every morning he went out with his umbrella and put a stick in the place where the water came up to, and every next morning he went out and couldn't see his stick any more, so he put another stick in the place where the water came up to, and then he walked home again, and each morning he had a shorter way to walk than he had had the morning before. On the morning of the fifth day he saw the water all round him, and knew that for the first time in his life he was on a real island. Which was very exciting.

It was on this morning that Owl came flying over the water to say "How do you do?" to his friend Christopher Robin.

"I say, Owl," said Christopher Robin, "isn't this fun? I'm on an island!"

"The atmospheric conditions have been very unfavourable lately," said Owl.

"The what?"

"It has been raining," explained Owl.

"Yes," said Christopher Robin. "It has."

"The flood-level has reached an unprecedented height."

"The who?"

"There's a lot of water about," explained Owl.

"Yes," said Christopher Robin, "there is."

"However, the prospects are rapidly becoming more favourable. At any moment —"

"Have you seen Pooh?"

"No. At any moment —"

"I hope he's all right," said Christopher Robin. "I've been wondering about him. I expect Piglet's with him. Do you think they're all right, Owl?"

"I expect so. You see, at any moment —"

"Do go and see, Owl. Because Pooh hasn't got very much brain, and he might do something silly, and I do love him so, Owl. Do you see, Owl?"

"That's all right," said Owl. "I'll go. Back directly." And he flew off.

In a little while he was back again.

"Pooh isn't there," he said.

"Not there?"

"He's *been* there. He's been sitting on a branch of his tree outside his house with nine pots of honey. But he isn't there now."

"Oh, Pooh!" cried Christopher Robin. "Where *are* you?"

"Here I am," said a growly voice behind him.

"Pooh!"

They rushed into each other's arms.

"How did you get here, Pooh?" asked Christopher Robin, when he was ready to talk again.

"On my boat," said Pooh proudly. "I had a Very Important Message sent me in a bottle, and owing to having got some water in my eyes, I couldn't read it, so I brought it to you. On my boat."

With these proud words he gave Christopher Robin the message.

"But it's from Piglet!" cried Christopher Robin when he had read it.

"Isn't there anything about Pooh in it?" asked Bear, looking over his shoulder.

Christopher Robin read the message aloud.

"Oh, are those 'P's' piglets? I thought they were poohs."

"We must rescue him at once! I thought he was with *you*, Pooh. Owl, could you rescue him on your back?"

"I don't think so," said Owl, after grave thought. "It is doubtful if the necessary dorsal muscles —"

"Then would you fly to him at *once* and say that Rescue is Coming? And Pooh and I will think of a Rescue and come as quick as ever we can. Oh, don't *talk*, Owl, go on quick!" And, still thinking of something to say, Owl flew off.

"Now then, Pooh," said Christopher Robin, "where's your boat?"

"I ought to say," explained Pooh as they walked down to the shore of the island, "that it isn't just an ordinary sort of boat. Sometimes it's a Boat, and sometimes it's more of an Accident. It all depends."

"Depends on what?"

"On whether I'm on the top of it or underneath it."

"Oh! Well, where is it?"

"There!" said Pooh, pointing proudly to *The Floating Bear.*

It wasn't what Christopher Robin expected, and the more he looked at it, the more he thought what a Brave and Clever Bear Pooh was, and the more Christopher Robin thought this, the more Pooh looked modestly down his nose and tried to pretend he wasn't.

"But it's too small for two of us," said Christopher Robin sadly.

"Three of us with Piglet."

"That makes it smaller still. Oh, Pooh Bear, what shall we do?"

And then this Bear, Pooh Bear, Winnie-the-Pooh, F.O.P. (Friend of Piglet's), R.C. (Rabbit's Companion), P.D. (Pole Discoverer), E.C. and T.F. (Eeyore's Comforter and Tail-finder) – in fact, Pooh himself – said something so clever that Christopher Robin could only look at him with mouth open and eyes staring, wondering if this was really the Bear of Very Little Brain whom he had known and loved so long.

"We might go in your umbrella," said Pooh.

"?"

"We might go in your umbrella," said Pooh.

"??"

"We might go in your umbrella," said Pooh.

"!!!!!!"

For suddenly Christopher Robin saw that they might. He opened his umbrella and put it point downwards in the water. It floated but wobbled. Pooh got in. He was just beginning to say that it was all right now, when he

found that it wasn't, so after a short drink, which he didn't really want, he waded back to Christopher Robin. Then they both got in together, and it wobbled no longer.

"I shall call this boat *The Brain of Pooh*," said Christopher Robin, and *The Brain of Pooh* set sail forthwith in a south-westerly direction, revolving gracefully.

You can imagine Piglet's joy when at last the ship came in sight of him.
In after-years he liked to think that he had been in Very Great Danger during
the Terrible Flood, but the only danger he had really been in was the last
half-hour of his imprisonment, when Owl, who had just flown up, sat on a
branch of his tree to comfort him, and told him a very long story about an
aunt who had once laid a seagull's egg by mistake, and the story went on and
on, rather like this sentence, until Piglet who was listening out of his window
without much hope, went to sleep quietly and naturally, slipping slowly out of
the window towards the water until he was only hanging on by his toes, at
which moment, luckily, a sudden loud squawk from Owl, which was really

part of the story, being what his aunt said, woke the Piglet up and just gave him time to jerk himself back into safety and say, "How interesting, and did she?" when – well you can imagine his joy when at last he saw the good ship, *The Brain of Pooh* (*Captain*, C. Robin; *1st Mate*, P. Bear) coming over the sea to rescue him. . . .

And as that is really the end of the story, and I am very tired after that last sentence, I think I shall stop there.

Down by the Pond

I'm fishing.
Don't talk, anybody, don't come near!
Can't you see that the fish might hear?
He thinks I'm playing with a piece of string;
He thinks I'm another sort of funny sort of thing,
    But he doesn't know I'm fishing –
    He doesn't know I'm fishing.
        That's what I'm doing –
          Fishing.

No, I'm not, I'm newting.
Don't cough, anybody, don't come by!
Any small noise makes a newt feel shy.
He thinks I'm a bush, or a new sort of tree;
He thinks it's somebody, but doesn't think it's Me.
    And he doesn't know I'm newting –
    No, he doesn't know I'm newting.
        That's what I'm doing –
            Newting.

Christopher Robin Gives a Party

One day when the sun had come back over the Forest, bringing with it the scent of may, and all the streams of the Forest were tinkling happily to find themselves their own pretty shape again, and the little pools lay dreaming of the life they had seen and the big things they had done, and in the warmth and quiet of the Forest the cuckoo was trying over his voice carefully and listening to see if he liked it, and wood-pigeons were complaining gently to themselves in their lazy comfortable way that it was the other fellow's fault, but it didn't matter very much; on such a day as this Christopher Robin whistled in a special way he had, and Owl came flying out of the Hundred Acre Wood to see what was wanted.

"Owl," said Christopher Robin, "I am going to give a party."

"You are, are you?" said Owl.

"And it's to be a special sort of party, because it's because of what Pooh did when he did what he did to save Piglet from the flood."

"Oh, that's what it's for, is it?" said Owl.

"Yes, so will you tell Pooh as quickly as you can, and all the others, because it will be tomorrow?"

"Oh, it will, will it?" said Owl, still being as helpful as possible.

"So will you go and tell them, Owl?"

Owl tried to think of something very wise to say, but couldn't, so he flew off to tell the others. And the first person he told was Pooh.

"Pooh," he said. "Christopher Robin is giving a party."

"Oh!" said Pooh. And then seeing that Owl expected him to say something else, he said, "Will there be those little cake things with pink sugar icing?"

Owl felt that it was rather beneath him to talk about little cake things with pink sugar icing, so he told Pooh exactly what Christopher Robin had said, and flew off to Eeyore.

"A party for Me?" thought Pooh to himself. "How grand!" And he began to wonder if all the other animals would know that it was a special Pooh Party, and if Christopher Robin had told them about *The Floating Bear* and *The Brain of Pooh* and all the wonderful ships he had invented and sailed on, and he began to think how awful it would be if everybody had forgotten about it, and nobody quite knew what the party was for; and the more he thought like this, the more the party got muddled in his mind, like a dream when nothing goes right. And the dream began to sing itself over in his head until it became a sort of song. It was an

ANXIOUS POOH SONG

3 Cheers for Pooh!
(*For who?*)
For Pooh –
(*Why what did he do?*)
I thought you knew;
He saved his friend from a wetting!
3 Cheers for Bear!

(*For where?*)
For Bear –
He couldn't swim,
But he rescued him!
(*He rescued who?*)
Oh, listen, do!
I am talking of Pooh –
(*Of who?*)
Of Pooh!

(*I'm sorry I keep forgetting*).
Well, Pooh was a Bear of Enormous Brain –
(*Just say it again!*)
Of enormous brain –
(*Of enormous what?*)

Well, he ate a lot,
And I don't know if he could swim or not,
But he managed to float
On a sort of boat
(*On a sort of what?*)
Well, a sort of pot –
So now let's give him three hearty cheers
(*So now let's give him three hearty whiches!*)
And hope he'll be with us for years and years,
And grow in health and wisdom and riches!
3 Cheers for Pooh!
(*For who?*)
For Pooh –
3 Cheers for Bear!
(*For where?*)
For Bear –
3 Cheers for the wonderful Winnie-the-Pooh!
(*Just tell me, somebody* – WHAT DID HE DO?)

While this was going on inside him, Owl was talking to Eeyore.

"Eeyore," said Owl, "Christopher Robin is giving a party."

"Very interesting," said Eeyore. "I suppose they will be sending me down the odd bits which got trodden on. Kind and Thoughtful. Not at all, don't mention it."

"There is an Invitation for you."

"What's that like?"

"An Invitation!"

"Yes, I heard you. Who dropped it?"

"This isn't anything to eat, it's asking you to the party. Tomorrow."

Eeyore shook his head slowly.

"You mean Piglet. The little fellow with the excited ears. That's Piglet. I'll tell him."

"No, no," said Owl, getting quite fussy. "It's you!"

"Are you sure?"

"Of course I'm sure. Christopher Robin said 'All of them! Tell all of them.'"

"All of them, except Eeyore?"

"All of them," said Owl sulkily.

"Ah!" said Eeyore. "A mistake, no doubt, but still, I shall come. Only don't blame *me* if it rains."

But it didn't rain. Christopher Robin had made a long table out of some long pieces of wood, and they all sat round it. Christopher Robin sat at one end, and Pooh sat at the other, and between them on one side were Owl and Eeyore and Piglet, and between them on the other side were Rabbit, and Roo and Kanga. And all Rabbit's friends-and-relations spread themselves about on the grass, and waited hopefully in case anybody spoke to them, or dropped anything, or asked them the time.

It was the first party to which Roo had ever been, and he was very excited. As soon as ever they had sat down he began to talk.

"Hallo, Pooh!" he squeaked.

"Hallo, Roo!" said Pooh.

Roo jumped up and down in his seat for a little while and then began again.

"Hallo, Piglet!" he squeaked.

Piglet waved a paw at him, being too busy to say anything.

"Hallo, Eeyore!" said Roo.

Eeyore nodded gloomily at him. "It will rain soon, you see if it doesn't," he said.

Roo looked to see if it didn't, and it didn't, so he said "Hallo, Owl!" – and Owl said "Hallo, my little fellow," in a kindly way, and went on telling Christopher Robin about an accident which had nearly happened to a friend of his whom Christopher Robin didn't know, and Kanga said to Roo, "Drink up your milk first, dear, and talk afterwards." So Roo, who was drinking his milk, tried to say that he could do both at once . . . and had to be patted on the back and dried for quite a long time afterwards.

When they had all nearly eaten enough, Christopher Robin banged on the table with his spoon, and everybody stopped talking and was very silent, except Roo who was just finishing a loud attack of hiccups and trying to look as if it was one of Rabbit's relations.

"This party," said Christopher Robin, "is a party because of what someone did, and we all know who it was, and it's his party, because of what he did, and I've got a present for him and here it is." Then he felt about a little and whispered, "Where is it?"

While he was looking, Eeyore coughed in an impressive way and began to speak.

"Friends," he said, "including oddments, it is a great pleasure, or perhaps I had better say it has been a pleasure so far, to see you at my party. What I did was nothing. Any of you – except Rabbit and Owl and Kanga – would have done the same. Oh, and Pooh. My remarks do not, of course, apply to Piglet and Roo, because they are too small. Any of you would have done the same. But it just happened to be Me. It was not, I need hardly say, with an idea of getting what Christopher Robin is looking for now" – and he put his front leg to his mouth and said in a loud whisper, "Try under the table" – "that I did what I did – but because I feel that we should all do what we can to help. I feel that we should all —"

"H–hup!" said Roo accidentally.

"Roo, dear!" said Kanga reproachfully.

"Was it me?" asked Roo, a little surprised.

"What's Eeyore talking about?" Piglet whispered to Pooh.

"I don't know," said Pooh rather dolefully.

"I thought this was *your* party."

"I thought it was *once*. But I suppose it isn't."

"I'd sooner it was yours than Eeyore's," said Piglet.

"So would I," said Pooh.

"H–hup!" said Roo again.

"AS – I – WAS – SAYING," said Eeyore loudly and sternly, "as I was saying when I was interrupted by various Loud Sounds, I feel that —"

"Here it is!" cried Christopher Robin excitedly. "Pass it down to silly old Pooh. It's for Pooh."

"For Pooh?" said Eeyore.

"Of course it is. The best bear in all the world."

"I might have known," said Eeyore. "After all, one can't complain. I have my friends. Somebody spoke to me only yesterday. And was it last week or the week before that Rabbit bumped into me and said 'Bother!' The Social Round. Always something going on."

Nobody was listening, for they were all saying, "Open it, Pooh," "What is it, Pooh?" "I know what it is," "No, you don't," and other helpful remarks of this sort. And of course Pooh was opening it as quickly as ever he could, but without cutting the string, because you never know when a bit of string might be Useful. At last it was undone.

When Pooh saw what it was, he nearly fell down, he was so pleased. It was a Special Pencil Case. There were pencils in it marked "B" for Bear, and pencils marked "HB" for Helping Bear, and pencils marked "BB" for Brave Bear. There was a knife for sharpening the pencils, and indiarubber for rubbing out anything which you had spelt wrong, and a ruler for ruling lines for the words to walk on, and inches marked on the ruler in case you wanted to know how many inches anything was, and Blue Pencils and Red Pencils and Green Pencils for saying special things in blue and red and green. And all these lovely things were in little pockets of their own in a Special Case which shut with a click when you clicked it. And they were all for Pooh.

"Oh!" said Pooh.

"Oh, Pooh!" said everybody else except Eeyore.

"Thank you," growled Pooh.

But Eeyore was saying to himself, "This writing business. Pencils and what-not. Over-rated, if you ask me. Silly stuff. Nothing in it."

Later on, when they had all said "Good-bye" and "Thank you" to

Christopher Robin, Pooh and Piglet walked home thoughtfully together in the golden evening, and for a long time they were silent.

"When you wake up in the morning, Pooh," said Piglet at last, "what's the first thing you say to yourself?"

"What's for breakfast?" said Pooh. "What do *you* say, Piglet?"

"I say, I wonder what's going to happen exciting *today?*" said Piglet.

Pooh nodded thoughtfully.

"It's the same thing," he said.

"And what did happen?" asked Christopher Robin.

"When?"

"Next morning."

"I don't know."

"Could you think, and tell me and Pooh sometime?"

"If you wanted it very much."

"Pooh does," said Christopher Robin.

He gave a deep sigh, picked his bear up by the leg and walked off to the door, trailing Winnie-the-Pooh behind him. At the door he turned and said, "Coming to see me have my bath?"

"I might," I said.

"Was Pooh's pencil case any better than mine?"

"It was just the same," I said.

He nodded and went out . . . and in a moment I heard Winnie-the-Pooh – *bump, bump, bump* – going up the stairs behind him.

WAITING AT THE WINDOW

These are my two drops of rain
Waiting on the window-pane.

I am waiting here to see
Which the winning one will be.

Both of them have different names.
One is John and one is James.

All the best and all the worst
Comes from which of them is first.

VESPERS

Little Boy kneels at the foot of the bed,
Droops on the little hands little gold head.
Hush! Hush! Whisper who dares!
Christopher Robin is saying his prayers.

God bless Mummy. I know that's right.
Wasn't it fun in the bath tonight?
The cold's so cold, and the hot's so hot.
Oh! *God bless Daddy* – I quite forgot.

If I open my fingers a little bit more,
I can see Nanny's dressing-gown on the door.
It's a beautiful blue, but it hasn't a hood.
Oh! *God bless Nanny and make her good.*

Mine has a hood, and I lie in bed,
And pull the hood right over my head,
And I shut my eyes, and I curl up small,
And nobody knows that I'm there at all.

Oh! *Thank you, God, for a lovely day.*
And what was the other I had to say?
I said "Bless Daddy," so what can it be?
Oh! Now I remember it. *God bless Me.*

Little Boy kneels at the foot of the bed,
Droops on the little hands little gold head.
Hush! Hush! Whisper who dares!
Christopher Robin is saying his prayers.

A House is Built for Eeyore

One day when Pooh Bear had nothing else to do, he thought he would do something, so he went round to Piglet's house to see what Piglet was doing. It was still snowing as he stumped over the white forest track, and he expected to find Piglet warming his toes in front of his fire, but to his surprise he saw that the door was open, and the more he looked inside the more Piglet wasn't there.

"He's out," said Pooh sadly. "That's what it is. He's not in. I shall have to go on a fast Thinking Walk by myself. Bother!"

But first he thought that he would knock very loudly just to make *quite* sure . . . and while he waited for Piglet not to answer, he jumped up and down to keep warm, and a hum came suddenly into his head, which seemed to him a Good Hum, such as is Hummed Hopefully to Others.

The more it snows
(Tiddely pom),
The more it goes
(Tiddely pom),
The more it goes
(Tiddely pom),
On snowing.
And nobody knows
(Tiddely pom),
How cold my toes
(Tiddely pom),
How cold my toes
(Tiddely pom),
Are growing.

"So what I'll do," said Pooh, "is I'll do this. I'll just go home first and see what the time is, and perhaps I'll put a muffler round my neck, and then I'll go and see Eeyore and sing it to him."

He hurried back to his own house; and his mind was so busy on the way with the hum that he was getting ready for Eeyore that, when he suddenly saw Piglet sitting in his best arm-chair, he could only stand there rubbing his head and wondering whose house he was in.

"Hallo, Piglet," he said. "I thought you were out."

"No," said Piglet, "it's you who were out, Pooh."

"So it was," said Pooh. "I knew one of us was."

He looked up at his clock, which had stopped at five minutes to eleven some weeks ago.

"Nearly eleven o'clock," said Pooh happily. "You're just in time for a little smackerel of something," and he put his head into the cupboard. "And then we'll go out, Piglet, and sing my song to Eeyore."

"Which song, Pooh?"

"The one we're going to sing to Eeyore," explained Pooh.

The clock was still saying five minutes to eleven when Pooh and Piglet set out on their way half an hour later. The wind had dropped, and the snow, tired of rushing round in circles trying to catch itself up, now fluttered gently down until it found a place on which to rest, and sometimes the place was Pooh's nose and sometimes it wasn't, and in a little while Piglet was wearing a white muffler round his neck and feeling more snowy behind the ears than he had ever felt before.

"Pooh," he said at last, and a little timidly, because he didn't want Pooh to think he was Giving In, "I was just wondering. How would it be if we went home now and *practised* your song, and then sang it to Eeyore tomorrow – or – or the next day, when we happen to see him?"

"That's a very good idea, Piglet," said Pooh. "We'll practise it now as we go along. But it's no good going home to practise it, because it's a special Outdoor Song which Has To Be Sung In The Snow."

"Are you sure?" asked Piglet anxiously.

"Well, you'll see, Piglet, when you listen. Because this is how it begins. *The more it snows, tiddely pom —*"

"Tiddely what?" said Piglet.

"Pom," said Pooh. "I put that in to make it more hummy. *The more it goes, tiddely pom, the more —*"

"Didn't you say snows?"

"Yes, but that was *before*."

"Before the tiddely *pom?*"

"It was a *different* tiddely pom," said Pooh, feeling rather muddled now. "I'll sing it to you properly and then you'll see."

So he sang it again.

> The more it
> SNOWS-tiddely-pom
> The more it
> GOES-tiddely-pom
> The more it
> GOES-tiddely-pom
> On
> Snowing.
>
> And nobody
> KNOWS-tiddely-pom,
> How cold my
> TOES-tiddely-pom
> How cold my
> TOES-tiddely-pom
> Are Growing.

He sang it like that, which is much the best way of singing it, and when he had finished, he waited for Piglet to say that, of all the Outdoor Hums for

Snowy Weather he had ever heard, this was the best. And, after thinking the matter out carefully, Piglet said:

"Pooh," he said solemnly, "it isn't the *toes* so much as the *ears*."

By this time they were getting near Eeyore's Gloomy Place, which was where he lived, and as it was still very snowy behind Piglet's ears, and he was getting tired of it, they turned into a little pine-wood, and sat down on the gate which led into it. They were out of the snow now, but it was very cold, and to keep themselves warm they sang Pooh's song right through six times, Piglet doing the tiddely-poms and Pooh doing the rest of it, and both of them thumping on the top of the gate with pieces of stick at the proper places.

And in a little while they felt much warmer, and were able to talk again.

"I've been thinking," said Pooh, "and what I've been thinking about is this. I've been thinking about Eeyore."

"What about Eeyore?"

"Well, poor Eeyore has nowhere to live."

"Nor he has," said Piglet.

"*You* have a house, Piglet, and I have a house, and they are very good houses. And Christopher Robin has a house, and Owl and Kanga and Rabbit have houses, and even Rabbit's friends and relations have houses or somethings, but poor Eeyore has nothing. So what I've been thinking is: Let's build him a house."

"That," said Piglet, "is a Grand Idea. Where shall we build it?"

"We will build it here," said Pooh, "just by this wood, out of the wind, because this is where I thought of it. And we will call this Pooh Corner. And we will build an Eeyore House with sticks at Pooh Corner for Eeyore."

"There was a heap of sticks on the other side of the wood," said Piglet. "I saw them. Lots and lots. All piled up."

"Thank you, Piglet," said Pooh. "What you have just said will be a Great Help to us, and because of it I could call this place Poohanpiglet Corner if Pooh Corner didn't sound better, which it does, being smaller and more like a corner. Come along."

So they got down off the gate and went round to the other side of the wood to fetch the sticks.

Christopher Robin had spent the morning indoors going to Africa and back, and he had just got off the boat and was wondering what it was like outside, when who should come knocking at the door but Eeyore.

"Hallo, Eeyore," said Christopher Robin, as he opened the door and came out. "How are *you?*"

"It's snowing still," said Eeyore gloomily.

"So it is."

"*And* freezing."

"Is it?"

"Yes," said Eeyore. "However," he said, brightening up a little, "we haven't had an earthquake lately."

"What's the matter, Eeyore?"

"Nothing, Christopher Robin. Nothing important. I suppose you haven't seen a house or what-not anywhere about?"

"What sort of a house?"

"Just a house."

"Who lives there?"

"I do. At least I thought I did. But I suppose I don't. After all, we can't all have houses."

"But, Eeyore, I didn't know – I always thought —"

"I don't know how it is, Christopher Robin, but what with all this snow and one thing and another, not to mention icicles and such-like, it isn't so Hot in my field about three o'clock in the morning as some people think it is. It isn't Close, if you know what I mean – not so as to be uncomfortable. It isn't Stuffy. In fact, Christopher Robin," he went on in a loud whisper, "quite-between-ourselves-and-don't-tell-anybody, it's Cold."

"Oh, Eeyore!"

"And I said to myself: The others will be sorry if I'm getting myself all cold. They haven't got Brains, any of them, only grey fluff that's blown into their heads by mistake, and they don't Think, but if it goes on snowing for another six weeks or so, one of them will begin to say to himself: 'Eeyore can't be so very much too Hot about three o'clock in the morning.' And then it will Get About. And they'll be Sorry."

"Oh, Eeyore!" said Christopher Robin, feeling very sorry already.

"I don't mean you, Christopher Robin. You're different. So what it all comes to is that I built myself a house down by my little wood."

"Did you really? How exciting!"

"The really exciting part," said Eeyore in his most melancholy voice, "is that when I left it this morning it was there, and when I came back it wasn't. Not at all, very natural, and it was only Eeyore's house. But still I just wondered."

Christopher Robin didn't stop to wonder. He was already back in *his* house, putting on his waterproof hat, his waterproof boots, and his waterproof macintosh as fast as he could.

"We'll go and look for it at once," he called out to Eeyore.

"Sometimes," said Eeyore, "when people have quite finished taking a person's house, there are one or two bits which they don't want and are rather glad for the person to take back, if you know what I mean. So I thought if we just went —"

"Come on," said Christopher Robin, and off they hurried, and in a very little time they got to the corner of the field by the side of the pine-wood, where Eeyore's house wasn't any longer.

"There!" said Eeyore. "Not a stick of it left! Of course, I've still got all this snow to do what I like with. One mustn't complain."

But Christopher Robin wasn't listening to Eeyore, he was listening to something else.

"Can you hear it?" he asked.

"What is it? Somebody laughing?"

"Listen."

They both listened . . . and they heard a deep gruff voice saying in a singing voice that the more it snowed the more it went on snowing, and a small high voice tiddely-pomming in between.

"It's Pooh," said Christopher Robin excitedly. . . .

"Possibly," said Eeyore.

"*And* Piglet!" said Christopher Robin excitedly.

"Probably," said Eeyore. "What we *want* is a Trained Bloodhound."

The words of the song changed suddenly.

"*We've finished our HOUSE!*" sang the gruff voice.

"*Tiddely pom!*" sang the squeaky one.

"*It's a beautiful* HOUSE . . ."

"*Tiddely pom . . .*"

"*I wish it were* MINE . . ."

"*Tiddely pom . . .*"

"Pooh!" shouted Christopher Robin. . . .

The singers on the gate stopped suddenly.

"It's Christopher Robin!" said Pooh eagerly.

"He's round by the place where we got all those sticks from," said Piglet.

"Come on," said Pooh.

They climbed down their gate and hurried round the corner of the wood, Pooh making welcoming noises all the way.

"Why, here *is* Eeyore," said Pooh, when he had finished hugging Christopher Robin, and he nudged Piglet, and Piglet nudged him, and they thought to themselves what a lovely surprise they had got ready. "Hallo, Eeyore."

"Same to you, Pooh Bear, and twice on Thursdays," said Eeyore gloomily.

Before Pooh could say: "Why Thursdays?" Christopher Robin began to explain the sad story of Eeyore's Lost House. And Pooh and Piglet listened, and their eyes seemed to get bigger and bigger.

"*Where* did you say it was?" asked Pooh.

"Just here," said Eeyore.

"Made of sticks?"

"Yes."

"Oh!" said Piglet.

"What?" said Eeyore.

"I just said 'Oh!'" said Piglet nervously. And so as to seem quite at ease he hummed tiddely pom once or twice in a what-shall-we-do-now kind of way.

"You're sure it *was* a house?" said Pooh. "I mean, you're sure the house was just here?"

"Of course I am," said Eeyore. And he murmured to himself, "No brain at all, some of them."

"Why, what's the matter, Pooh?" asked Christopher Robin.

"Well," said Pooh . . . "The fact *is*," said Pooh . . . "Well, the fact *is*," said Pooh . . . "You see," said Pooh . . . "It's like this," said Pooh, and something seemed to tell him that he wasn't explaining very well, and he nudged Piglet again.

"It's like this," said Piglet quickly. . . . "Only warmer," he added after deep thought.

"What's warmer?"

"The other side of the wood, where Eeyore's house is."

"My house?" said Eeyore. "My house was here."

"No," said Piglet firmly. "The other side of the wood."

"Because of being warmer," said Pooh.

"But I ought to *know* —"

"Come and look," said Piglet simply, and he led the way.

"There wouldn't be *two* houses," said Pooh. "Not so close together."

They came round the corner, and there was Eeyore's house, looking as comfy as anything.

"There you are," said Piglet.

"Inside as well as outside," said Pooh proudly.

Eeyore went inside . . . and came out again.

"It's a remarkable thing," he said. "It *is* my house, and I built it where I said I did, so the wind must have blown it here. And the wind blew it right over the wood, and blew it down here, and here it is as good as ever. In fact, better in places."

"Much better," said Pooh and Piglet together.

"It just shows what can be done by taking a little trouble," said Eeyore. "Do you see, Pooh? Do you see, Piglet? Brains first and then Hard Work. Look at it! *That's* the way to build a house," said Eeyore proudly.

So they left him in it; and Christopher Robin went back to lunch with his friends Pooh and Piglet, and on the way they told him of the Awful Mistake they had made. And when he had finished laughing, they all sang the Outdoor Song for Snowy Weather the rest of the way home, Piglet, who was still not quite sure of his voice, putting in the tiddely-poms again.

"And I know it *seems* easy," said Piglet to himself, "but it isn't *every one* who could do it."

SNEEZLES

Christopher Robin
Had wheezles
And sneezles,
They bundled him
Into
His bed.
They gave him what goes
With a cold in the nose,
And some more for a cold
In the head.
They wondered
If wheezles
Could turn
Into measles,
If sneezles
Would turn
Into mumps;
They examined his chest
For a rash,
And the rest
Of his body for swellings and lumps.
They sent for some doctors
In sneezles
And wheezles
To tell them what ought
To be done.

All sorts and conditions
Of famous physicians
Came hurrying round
At a run.
They all made a note
Of the state of his throat,
They asked if he suffered from thirst;
They asked if the sneezles
Came *after* the wheezles,
Or if the first sneezle
Came first.
They said, "If you teazle
A sneezle
Or wheezle,
A measle
May easily grow.
But humour or pleazle
The wheezle
Or sneezle,
The measle
Will certainly go."

They expounded the reazles
For sneezles
And wheezles,
The manner of measles
When new.
They said "If he freezles
In draughts and in breezles,
Then PHTHEEZLES
May even ensue."

Christopher Robin
Got up in the morning,
The sneezles had vanished away.
And the look in his eye
Seemed to say to the sky,
"Now, how to amuse them today?"

FURRY BEAR

If I were a bear,
  And a big bear too,
I shouldn't much care
  If it froze or snew;
I shouldn't much mind
  If it snowed or friz –
I'd be all fur-lined
  With a coat like his!

For I'd have fur boots and a brown fur wrap,
And brown fur knickers and a big fur cap.
I'd have a fur muffle-ruff to cover my jaws,
And brown fur mittens on my big brown paws.
With a big brown furry-down up to my head,
I'd sleep all the winter in a big fur bed.

TIGGER COMES TO THE FOREST
AND HAS BREAKFAST

Winnie-the-Pooh woke up suddenly in the middle of the night and listened. Then he got out of bed, and lit his candle, and stumped across the room to see if anybody was trying to get into his honey-cupboard, and they weren't, so he stumped back again, blew out his candle, and got into bed. Then he heard the noise again.

"Is that you, Piglet?" he said.

But it wasn't.

"Come in, Christopher Robin," he said.

But Christopher Robin didn't.

"Tell me about it tomorrow, Eeyore," said Pooh sleepily.

But the noise went on.

"*Worraworraworraworraworra*," said Whatever-it-was, and Pooh found that he wasn't asleep after all.

"What can it be?" he thought. "There are lots of noises in the Forest, but this is a different one. It isn't a growl, and it isn't a purr, and it isn't a bark, and it isn't the noise-you-make-before-beginning-a-piece-of-poetry, but it's a noise of some kind, made by a strange animal! And he's making it outside my door. So I shall get up and ask him not to do it."

He got out of bed and opened his front door.

"Hallo!" said Pooh, in case there was anything outside.

"Hallo!" said Whatever-it-was.

"Oh!" said Pooh. "Hallo!"

"Hallo!"

"Oh, *there* you are!" said Pooh. "Hallo!"

"Hallo!" said the Strange Animal, wondering how long this was going on.

Pooh was just going to say "Hallo!" for the fourth time when he thought that he wouldn't, so he said, "Who is it?" instead.

"Me," said a voice.

"Oh!" said Pooh. "Well, come here."

So Whatever-it-was came here, and in the light of the candle he and Pooh looked at each other.

"I'm Pooh," said Pooh.

"I'm Tigger," said Tigger.

"Oh!" said Pooh, for he had never seen an animal like this before. "Does Christopher Robin know about you?"

"Of course he does," said Tigger.

"Well," said Pooh, "it's the middle of the night, which is a good time for going to sleep. And tomorrow morning we'll have some honey for breakfast. Do Tiggers like honey?"

"They like everything," said Tigger cheerfully.

"Then if they like going to sleep on the floor, I'll go back to bed," said Pooh, "and we'll do things in the morning. Good night." And he got back into bed and went fast asleep.

When he awoke in the morning, the first thing he saw was Tigger, sitting in front of the glass and looking at himself.

"Hallo!" said Pooh.

"Hallo!" said Tigger. "I've found somebody just like me. I thought I was the only one of them."

Pooh got out of bed, and began to explain what a looking-glass was, but just as he was getting to the interesting part, Tigger said:

"Excuse me a moment, but there's something climbing up your table," and with one loud *Worraworraworraworraworra* he jumped at the end of the table-cloth, pulled it to the ground, wrapped himself up in it three times, rolled to the other end of the room, and, after a terrible struggle, got his head into the daylight again, and said cheerfully: "Have I won?"

"That's my table-cloth," said Pooh, as he began to unwind Tigger.

"I wondered what it was," said Tigger.

"It goes on the table and you put things on it."

"Then why did it try to bite me when I wasn't looking?"

"I don't *think* it did," said Pooh.

"It tried," said Tigger, "but I was too quick for it."

Pooh put the cloth back on the table, and he put a large honey-pot on the cloth, and they sat down to breakfast. And as soon as they sat down, Tigger took a large mouthful of honey . . . and he looked up at the ceiling with his head on one side, and made exploring noises with his tongue, and considering noises, and what-have-we-got-*here* noises . . . and then he said in a very decided voice:

"Tiggers don't like honey."

"Oh!" said Pooh, and tried to make it sound Sad and Regretful. "I thought they liked everything."

"Everything except honey," said Tigger.

Pooh felt rather pleased about this, and said that, as soon as he had finished his own breakfast, he would take Tigger round to Piglet's house, and Tigger could try some of Piglet's haycorns.

"Thank you, Pooh," said Tigger, "because haycorns is really what Tiggers like best."

So after breakfast they went round to see Piglet, and Pooh explained as they went that Piglet was a Very Small Animal who didn't like bouncing, and asked Tigger not to be too Bouncy just at first. And Tigger, who had been hiding behind trees and jumping out on Pooh's shadow when it wasn't looking, said that Tiggers were only bouncy before breakfast, and that as soon as they had had a few haycorns they became Quiet and Refined. So by-and-by they knocked at the door of Piglet's house.

"Hallo, Pooh," said Piglet.

"Hallo, Piglet. This is Tigger."

"Oh, is it?" said Piglet, and he edged round to the other side of the table. "I thought Tiggers were smaller than that."

"Not the big ones," said Tigger.

"They like haycorns," said Pooh, "so that's what we've come for, because poor Tigger hasn't had any breakfast yet."

Piglet pushed the bowl of haycorns towards Tigger, and said, "Help yourself," and then he got close up to Pooh and felt much braver, and said, "So you're Tigger? Well, well!" in a careless sort of voice. But Tigger said nothing because his mouth was full of haycorns. . . .

After a long munching noise he said:

"Ee-ers o i a-ors."

And when Pooh and Piglet said "What?" he said "Skoos ee," and went outside for a moment.

When he came back he said firmly:

"Tiggers don't like haycorns."

"But you said they liked everything except honey," said Pooh.

"Everything except honey *and* haycorns," explained Tigger.

When he heard this, Pooh said, "Oh, I see!" and Piglet, who was rather glad that Tiggers didn't like haycorns, said, "What about thistles?"

"Thistles," said Tigger, "is what Tiggers like best."

"Then let's go along and see Eeyore," said Piglet.

So the three of them went; and after they had walked and walked and walked, they came to the part of the Forest where Eeyore was.

"Hallo, Eeyore!" said Pooh. "This is Tigger."

"What is?" said Eeyore.

"This," explained Pooh and Piglet together, and Tigger smiled his happiest smile and said nothing.

Eeyore walked all round Tigger one way, and then turned and walked all round him the other way.

"What did you say it was?" he asked.

"Tigger."

"Ah!" said Eeyore.

"He's just come," explained Piglet.

"Ah!" said Eeyore again.

He thought for a long time and then said:

"When is he going?"

Pooh explained to Eeyore that Tigger was a great friend of Christopher Robin's, who had come to stay in the Forest, and Piglet explained to Tigger that he mustn't mind what Eeyore said because he was *always* gloomy; and Eeyore explained to Piglet that, on the contrary, he was feeling particularly cheerful this morning; and Tigger explained to anybody who was listening that he hadn't had any breakfast yet.

"I knew there was something," said Pooh. "Tiggers always eat thistles, so that was why we came to see you, Eeyore."

"Don't mention it, Pooh."

"Oh, Eeyore, I didn't mean that I didn't *want* to see you —"

"Quite – quite. But your new stripy friend – naturally, he wants his breakfast. What did you say his name was?"

"Tigger."

"Then come this way, Tigger."

Eeyore led the way to the most thistly-looking patch of thistles that ever was, and waved a hoof at it.

"A little patch I was keeping for my birthday," he said, "but, after all, what *are* birthdays? Here today and gone tomorrow. Help yourself, Tigger."

Tigger thanked him and looked a little anxiously at Pooh.

"Are these really thistles?" he whispered.

"Yes," said Pooh.

"What Tiggers like best?"

"That's right," said Pooh.

"I see," said Tigger.

So he took a large mouthful, and he gave a large crunch.

"*Ow!*" said Tigger.

He sat down and put his paw in his mouth.

"What's the matter?" asked Pooh.

"*Hot!*" mumbled Tigger.

"Your friend," said Eeyore, "appears to have bitten on a bee."

Pooh's friend stopped shaking his head to get the prickles out, and explained that Tiggers didn't like thistles.

"Then why bend a perfectly good one?" asked Eeyore.

"But you said," began Pooh, "– you *said* that Tiggers liked everything except honey and haycorns."

"*And* thistles," said Tigger, who was now running round in circles with his tongue hanging out.

Pooh looked at him sadly.

"What are we going to do?" he asked Piglet.

Piglet knew the answer to that, and he said at once that they must go and see Christopher Robin.

"You'll find him with Kanga," said Eeyore. He came close to Pooh, and said in a loud whisper:

"*Could* you ask your friend to do his exercises somewhere else? I shall be having lunch directly, and don't want it bounced on just before I begin. A trifling matter, and fussy of me, but we all have our little ways."

Pooh nodded solemnly and called to Tigger.

"Come along and we'll go and see Kanga. She's sure to have lots of breakfast for you."

Tigger finished his last circle and came up to Pooh and Piglet.

"Hot!" he explained with a large and friendly smile. "Come on!" and he rushed off.

Pooh and Piglet walked slowly after him. And as they walked Piglet said nothing, because he couldn't think of anything, and Pooh said nothing, because he was thinking of a poem. And when he had thought of it he began:

> What shall we do about poor little Tigger?
> If he never eats nothing he'll never get bigger.
> He doesn't like honey and haycorns and thistles
> Because of the taste and because of the bristles.
> And all the good things which an animal likes
> Have the wrong sort of swallow or too many spikes.

"He's quite big enough anyhow," said Piglet.
"He isn't *really* very big."
"Well, he *seems* so."
Pooh was thoughtful when he heard this, and then he murmured to himself:

> But whatever his weight in pounds, shillings, and
>   ounces,
> He always seems bigger because of his bounces.

"And that's the whole poem," he said. "Do you like it, Piglet?"
"All except the shillings," said Piglet. "I don't think they ought to be there."
"They wanted to come in after the pounds," explained Pooh, "so I let them. It is the best way to write poetry, letting things come."
"Oh, I didn't know," said Piglet.
Tigger had been bouncing in front of them all this time, turning round every now and then to ask, "Is this the way?" – and now at last they came in sight of Kanga's house, and there was Christopher Robin. Tigger rushed up to him.

"Oh, there you are, Tigger!" said Christopher Robin. "I knew you'd be somewhere."

"I've been finding things in the Forest," said Tigger importantly. "I've found a pooh and a piglet and an eeyore, but I can't find any breakfast."

Pooh and Piglet came up and hugged Christopher Robin, and explained what had been happening.

"Don't *you* know what Tiggers like?" asked Pooh.

"I expect if I thought very hard I should," said Christopher Robin, "but I *thought* Tigger knew."

"I do," said Tigger. "Everything there is in the world except honey and haycorns and – what were those hot things called?"

"Thistles."

"Yes, and those."

"Oh, well then, Kanga can give you some breakfast."

So they went into Kanga's house, and when Roo had said, "Hallo, Pooh," and "Hallo, Piglet" once, and "Hallo, Tigger" twice, because he had never said it before and it sounded funny, they told Kanga what they wanted, and Kanga said very kindly, "Well, look in my cupboard, Tigger dear, and see what you'd like." Because she knew at once that, however big Tigger seemed to be, he wanted as much kindness as Roo.

"Shall I look, too?" said Pooh, who was beginning to feel a little eleven o'clockish. And he found a small tin of condensed milk, and something

seemed to tell him that Tiggers didn't like this, so he took it into a corner by itself, and went with it to see that nobody interrupted it.

But the more Tigger put his nose into this and his paw into that, the more things he found which Tiggers didn't like. And when he had found everything in the cupboard, and couldn't eat any of it, he said to Kanga, "What happens now?"

But Kanga and Christopher Robin and

Piglet were all standing round Roo, watching him have his Extract of Malt. And Roo was saying, "Must I?" and Kanga was saying, "Now, Roo dear, you remember what you promised."

"What is it?" whispered Tigger to Piglet.

"His Strengthening Medicine," said Piglet. "He hates it."

So Tigger came closer, and he leant over the back of Roo's chair, and suddenly he put out his tongue, and took one large golollop, and, with a sudden jump of surprise, Kanga said, "Oh!" and then clutched at the spoon again just as it was disappearing, and pulled it safely back out of Tigger's mouth. But the Extract of Malt had gone.

"Tigger *dear*!" said Kanga.

"He's taken my medicine, he's taken my medicine, he's taken my medicine!" sang Roo happily, thinking it was a tremendous joke.

Then Tigger looked up at the ceiling, and closed his eyes, and his tongue went round and round his chops, in case he had left any outside, and a peaceful smile came over his face as he said, "So *that's* what Tiggers like!"

Which explains why he always lived at Kanga's house afterwards, and had Extract of Malt for breakfast, dinner, and tea. And sometimes, when Kanga thought he wanted strengthening, he had a spoonful or two of Roosbreakfast after meals as medicine.

"But *I* think," said Piglet to Pooh, "that he's been strengthened quite enough."

RICE PUDDING

What is the matter with Mary Jane?
She's crying with all her might and main,
And she won't eat her dinner – rice pudding again –
What *is* the matter with Mary Jane?

What is the matter with Mary Jane?
I've promised her dolls and a daisy-chain,
And a book about animals – all in vain –
What *is* the matter with Mary Jane?

What is the matter with Mary Jane?
She's perfectly well, and she hasn't a pain;
But, look at her, now she's beginning again! –
What *is* the matter with Mary Jane?

What is the matter with Mary Jane?
I've promised her sweets and a ride in the train,
And I've begged her to stop for a bit and explain –
What *is* the matter with Mary Jane?

What is the matter with Mary Jane?
She's perfectly well, and she hasn't a pain,
And it's lovely rice pudding for dinner again! –
What *is* the matter with Mary Jane?

Tiggers Don't Climb Trees

One day when Pooh was thinking, he thought he would go and see Eeyore, because he hadn't seen him since yesterday. And as he walked through the heather, singing to himself, he suddenly remembered that he hadn't seen Owl since the day before yesterday, so he thought that he would just look in at the Hundred Acre Wood on the way and see if Owl was at home.

Well, he went on singing, until he came to the part of the stream where the stepping-stones were, and when he was in the middle of the third stone he began to wonder how Kanga and Roo and Tigger were getting on, because they all lived together in a different part of the Forest. And he thought, "I haven't seen Roo for a long time, and if I don't see him today it will be a still longer time." So he sat down on the stone in the middle of the stream, and sang another verse of his song, while he wondered what to do. The other verse of the song was like this:

> I could spend a happy morning
> 　　Seeing Roo,
> I could spend a happy morning
> 　　Being Pooh.
> For it doesn't seem to matter,
> If I don't get any fatter
> (And I *don't* get any fatter),
> 　　What I do.

The sun was so delightfully warm, and the stone, which had been sitting in it for a long time, was so warm, too, that Pooh had almost decided to go on being Pooh in the middle of the stream for the rest of the morning, when he remembered Rabbit.

"Rabbit," said Pooh to himself. "I *like* talking to Rabbit. He talks about sensible things. He doesn't use long, difficult words, like Owl. He uses short, easy words, like 'What about lunch?' and 'Help yourself, Pooh.' I suppose, *really*, I ought to go and see Rabbit."

Which made him think of another verse:

> Oh, I like his way of talking,
>   Yes, I do.
> It's the nicest way of talking
>   Just for two.
> And a Help-yourself with Rabbit
> Though it may become a habit,
> Is a pleasant sort of habit
>   For a Pooh.

So when he had sung this, he got up off his stone, walked back across the stream, and set off for Rabbit's house.

But he hadn't got far before he began to say to himself:

"Yes, but suppose Rabbit is out?"

"Or suppose I get stuck in his front door again, coming out, as I did once when his front door wasn't big enough?"

"Because I *know* I'm not getting fatter, but his front door may be getting thinner."

"So wouldn't it be better if —"

And all the time he was saying things like this he was going more and more westerly, without thinking . . . until suddenly he found himself at his own front door again.

And it was eleven o'clock.

Which was Time-for-a-little-something. . . .

Half an hour later he was doing what he had always really meant to do, he was stumping off to Piglet's house. And as he walked, he wiped his mouth with the back of his paw, and sang rather a fluffy song through the fur.

It went like this:

> I could spend a happy morning
>> Seeing Piglet.
> And I couldn't spend a happy morning
>> Not seeing Piglet.
> And it doesn't seem to matter
> If I don't see Owl and Eeyore (or any of the others),
> And I'm not going to see Owl or Eeyore (or any of the others)
>> Or Christopher Robin.

Written down like this, it doesn't seem a very good song, but coming through pale fawn fluff at about half-past eleven on a very sunny morning, it seemed to Pooh to be one of the best songs he had ever sung. So he went on singing it.

Piglet was busy digging a small hole in the ground outside his house.

"Hallo, Piglet," said Pooh.

"Hallo, Pooh," said Piglet, giving a jump of surprise. "I knew it was you."

"So did I," said Pooh. "What are you doing?"

"I'm planting a haycorn, Pooh, so that it can grow up into an oak-tree, and have lots of haycorns just outside the front door instead of having to walk miles and miles, do you see, Pooh?"

"Supposing it doesn't?" said Pooh.

"It will, because Christopher Robin says it will, so that's why I'm planting it."

"Well," said Pooh, "if I plant a honeycomb outside my house, then it will grow up into a beehive."

Piglet wasn't quite sure about this.

"Or a *piece* of a honeycomb," said Pooh, "so as not to waste too much. Only then I might only get a piece of a beehive, and it might be the wrong piece, where the bees were buzzing and not hunnying. Bother."

Piglet agreed that that would be rather bothering.

"Besides, Pooh, it's a very difficult thing, planting, unless you know how to do it," he said; and he put the acorn in the hole he had made,

and covered it up with earth,

and jumped on it.

"I do know," said Pooh, "because Christopher Robin gave me a mastershalum seed, and I planted it, and I'm going to have mastershalums all over the front door."

"I thought they were called nasturtiums," said Piglet timidly, as he went on jumping.

"No," said Pooh. "Not these. These are called mastershalums."

When Piglet had finished jumping, he wiped his paws on his front, and said, "What shall we do now?" and Pooh said, "Let's go and see Kanga and Roo and Tigger," and Piglet said, "Y-yes. L-lets" – because he was still a little anxious about Tigger, who was a very Bouncy Animal, with a way of saying How-do-you-do, which always left your ears full of sand, even after Kanga had said, "Gently, Tigger dear," and had helped you up again. So they set off for Kanga's house.

Now it happened that Kanga had felt rather motherly that morning, and Wanting to Count Things – like Roo's vests, and how many pieces of soap there were left, and the two clean spots in Tigger's feeder; so she had sent them out with a packet of watercress sandwiches for Roo and a packet of extract-of-malt sandwiches for Tigger, to have a nice long morning in the Forest not getting into mischief. And off they had gone.

And as they went, Tigger told Roo (who wanted to know) all about the things that Tiggers could do.

"Can they fly?" asked Roo.

"Yes," said Tigger, "they're very good flyers, Tiggers are. Strornry good flyers."

"Oo!" said Roo. "Can they fly as well as Owl?"

"Yes," said Tigger. "Only they don't want to."

"Why don't they want to?"

"Well, they just don't like it, somehow."

Roo couldn't understand this, because he thought it would be lovely to be able to fly, but Tigger said it was difficult to explain to anybody who wasn't a Tigger himself.

"Well," said Roo, "can they jump as far as Kangas?"

"Yes," said Tigger. "When they want to."

"I *love* jumping," said Roo. "Let's see who can jump farthest, you or me."

"*I* can," said Tigger. "But we mustn't stop now, or we shall be late."

"Late for what?"

"For whatever we want to be in time for," said Tigger, hurrying on.

In a little while they came to the Six Pine Trees.

"I can swim," said Roo. "I fell into the river, and I swimmed. Can Tiggers swim?"

"Of course they can. Tiggers can do everything."

"Can they climb trees better than Pooh?" asked Roo, stopping under the tallest Pine Tree, and looking up at it.

"Climbing trees is what they do best," said Tigger. "Much better than Poohs."

"Could they climb this one?"

"They're always climbing trees like that," said Tigger. "Up and down all day."

"Oo, Tigger, are they *really?*"

"I'll show you," said Tigger bravely, "and you can sit on my back and watch me." For of all the things which he had said Tiggers could do, the only one he felt really certain about suddenly was climbing trees.

"Oo, Tigger – oo, Tigger – oo, Tigger!" squeaked Roo excitedly.

So he sat on Tigger's back and up they went.

And for the first ten feet Tigger said happily to himself, "Up we go!"

And for the next ten feet he said:

"I always *said* Tiggers could climb trees."

And for the next ten feet he said:

"Not that it's easy, mind you."

And for the next ten feet he said:

"Of course, there's the coming-down too. Backwards."

And then he said:

"Which will be difficult . . ."

"Unless one fell . . ."

"When it would be . . ."

"EASY."

And at the word "easy", the branch he was standing on broke suddenly and he just managed to clutch at the one above him as he felt himself going . . . and then slowly he got his chin over it . . . and then one back paw . . . and then the other . . . until at last he was sitting on it, breathing very quickly, and wishing that he had gone in for swimming instead.

Roo climbed off, and sat down next to him.

"Oo, Tigger," he said excitedly, "are we at the top?"

"No," said Tigger.

"Are we going to the top?"

"*No*," said Tigger.

"Oh!" said Roo rather sadly. And then he went on hopefully: "That was a lovely bit just now, when you pretended we were going to fall-bump-to-the-bottom, and we didn't. Will you do that bit again?"

"NO," said Tigger.

Roo was silent for a little while, and then he said, "Shall we eat our sandwiches, Tigger?" And Tigger said, "Yes, where are they?" And Roo said, "At the bottom of the tree." And Tigger said, "I don't think we'd better eat them just yet." So they didn't.

By-and-by Pooh and Piglet came along. Pooh was telling Piglet in a singing voice that it didn't seem to matter, if he didn't get any fatter, and he didn't *think* he was getting any fatter, what he did; and Piglet was wondering how long it would be before his haycorn came up.

"Look, Pooh!" said Piglet suddenly. "There's something in one of the Pine Trees."

"So there is!" said Pooh, looking up wonderingly. "There's an Animal."

Piglet took Pooh's arm, in case Pooh was frightened.

"Is it One of the Fiercer Animals?" he said, looking the other way.

Pooh nodded.

"It's a Jagular," he said.

"What do Jagulars do?" asked Piglet, hoping that they wouldn't.

"They hide in the branches of trees, and drop on you as you go underneath," said Pooh. "Christopher Robin told me."

"Perhaps we better hadn't go underneath, Pooh. In case he dropped and hurt himself."

TIGGERS DON'T CLIMB TREES

"They don't hurt themselves," said Pooh. "They're such very good droppers."

Piglet still felt that to be underneath a Very Good Dropper would be a Mistake, and he was just going to hurry back for something which he had forgotten when the Jagular called out to them.

"Help! Help!" it called.

"That's what Jagulars always do," said Pooh, much interested. "They call 'Help! Help!' and then when you look up, they drop on you."

"I'm looking *down*," cried Piglet loudly, so as the Jagular shouldn't do the wrong thing by accident.

Something very excited next to the Jagular heard him and squeaked:

"Pooh and Piglet! Pooh and Piglet!"

All of a sudden Piglet felt that it was a much nicer day than he had thought it was. All warm and sunny —

"Pooh!" he cried. "I believe it's Tigger and Roo!"

"So it is," said Pooh. "I thought it was a Jagular and another Jagular."

"Hallo, Roo!" called Piglet. "What are you doing?"

"We can't get down, we can't get down!" cried Roo. "Isn't it fun? Pooh, isn't it fun, Tigger and I are living in a tree, like Owl, and we're going to stay here for ever and ever. I can see Piglet's house. Piglet, I can see your house from here. Aren't we high? Is Owl's house as high up as this?"

"How did you get there, Roo?" asked Piglet.

"On Tigger's back! And Tiggers can't climb downwards, because their tails get in the way, only upwards, and Tigger forgot about that when we started, and he's only just remembered. So we've got to stay here for ever and ever – unless we go higher. What did you say, Tigger? Oh, Tigger says if we go higher we shan't be able to see Piglet's house so well, so we're going to stop here."

"Piglet," said Pooh solemnly, when he had heard all this, "what shall we do?" And he began to eat Tigger's sandwiches.

"Are they stuck?" asked Piglet anxiously.

Pooh nodded.

"Couldn't you climb up to them?"

"I might, Piglet, and I might bring Roo down on my back, but I couldn't bring Tigger down. So we must think of something else." And in a thoughtful way he began to eat Roo's sandwiches, too.

Whether he would have thought of anything before he had finished the last sandwich, I don't know, but he had just got to the last but one when there was a crackling in the bracken, and Christopher Robin and Eeyore came strolling along together.

"I shouldn't be surprised if it hailed a good deal tomorrow," Eeyore was saying. "Blizzards and what-not. Being fine today doesn't Mean Anything. It has no sig – what's that word? Well, it has none of that. It's just a small piece of weather."

"There's Pooh!" said Christopher Robin, who didn't much mind *what* it did tomorrow, as long as he was out in it. "Hallo, Pooh!"

"It's Christopher Robin!" said Piglet. "*He'll* know what to do."

They hurried up to him.

"Oh, Christopher Robin," began Pooh.

"And Eeyore," said Eeyore.

"Tigger and Roo are right up the Six Pine Trees, and they can't get down, and —"

"And I was just saying," put in Piglet, "that if only Christopher Robin —"

"*And* Eeyore —"

"If only you were here, then we could think of something to do."

Christopher Robin looked up at Tigger and Roo, and tried to think of something.

"*I* thought," said Piglet earnestly, "that if Eeyore stood at the bottom of the tree, and if Pooh stood on Eeyore's back, and if I stood on Pooh's shoulders —"

"And if Eeyore's back snapped suddenly, then we could all laugh. Ha Ha! Amusing in a quiet way," said Eeyore, "but not really helpful."

"Well," said Piglet meekly, "*I* thought —"

"Would it break your back, Eeyore?" asked Pooh, very much surprised.

"That's what would be so interesting, Pooh. Not being quite sure till afterwards."

Pooh said "Oh!" and they all began to think again.

"I've got an idea!" cried Christopher Robin suddenly.

"Listen to this, Piglet," said Eeyore, "and then you'll know what we're trying to do."

"I'll take off my tunic and we'll each hold a corner, and then Roo and Tigger can jump into it, and it will be all soft and bouncy for them, and they won't hurt themselves."

"*Getting Tigger down,*" said Eeyore, "and *Not hurting anybody*. Keep those two ideas in your head, Piglet, and you'll be all right."

But Piglet wasn't listening, he was so agog at the thought of seeing Christopher Robin's blue braces again. He had only seen them once before, when he was much younger, and, being a little over-excited by them, had had to go to bed half an hour earlier than usual; and he had always wondered since if they were *really* as blue and as bracing as he had thought them. So when Christopher Robin took his tunic off, and they were, he felt quite friendly to Eeyore again, and held the corner of the tunic next to him and smiled happily at him. And Eeyore whispered back: "I'm not saying there won't be an Accident *now*, mind you. They're funny things, Accidents. You never have them till you're having them."

When Roo understood what he had to do, he was wildly excited, and cried out: "Tigger, Tigger, we're going to jump! Look at me jumping, Tigger! Like

flying, my jumping will be. Can Tiggers do it?" And he squeaked out: "I'm coming, Christopher Robin!" and he jumped – straight into the middle of the tunic. And he was going so fast that he bounced up again almost as high as where he was before – and went on bouncing and saying "Oo!" for quite a long time – and then at last he stopped and said, "Oo, lovely!" And they put him on the ground.

"Come on, Tigger," he called out. "It's easy."

But Tigger was holding on to the branch and saying to himself: "It's all very well for Jumping Animals like Kangas, but it's quite different for Swimming Animals like Tiggers." And he thought of himself floating on his back down a river, or striking out from one island to another, and he felt that that was really the life for a Tigger.

"Come along," called Christopher Robin. "You'll be all right."

"Just wait a moment," said Tigger nervously. "Small piece of bark in my eye." And he moved slowly along his branch.

"Come on, it's easy!" squeaked Roo. And suddenly Tigger found how easy it was.

"Ow!" he shouted as the tree flew past him.

"Look out!" cried Christopher Robin to the others.

There was a crash, and a tearing noise, and a confused heap of everybody on the ground.

Christopher Robin and Pooh and Piglet picked themselves up first, and then they picked Tigger up, and underneath everybody else was Eeyore.

"Oh, Eeyore!" cried Christopher Robin. "Are you hurt?" And he felt him rather anxiously, and dusted him and helped him to stand up again.

Eeyore said nothing for a long time. And then he said: "Is Tigger there?"

Tigger was there, feeling Bouncy again already.

"Yes," said Christopher Robin. "Tigger's here."

"Well, just thank him for me," said Eeyore.

Halfway Down

Halfway down the stairs
Is a stair
Where I sit.
There isn't any
Other stair
Quite like
It.
I'm not at the bottom,
I'm not at the top;
So this is the stair
Where
I always
Stop.

Halfway up the stairs
Isn't up,
And isn't down.
It isn't in the nursery,
It isn't in the town.
And all sorts of funny thoughts
Run round my head:
"It isn't really
Anywhere!
It's somewhere else
Instead!"

Rabbit has a Busy Day

It was going to be one of Rabbit's busy days. As soon as he woke up he felt important, as if everything depended upon him. It was just the day for Organizing Something, or for Writing a Notice Signed Rabbit, or for Seeing What Everybody Else Thought About It. It was a perfect morning for hurrying round to Pooh, and saying, "Very well, then, I'll tell Piglet," and then going to Piglet, and saying, "Pooh thinks – but perhaps I'd better see Owl first." It was a Captainish sort of day, when everybody said, "Yes, Rabbit" and "No, Rabbit," and waited until he had told them.

He came out of his house and sniffed the warm spring morning as he wondered what he would do. Kanga's house was nearest, and at Kanga's house was Roo, who said "Yes, Rabbit" and "No, Rabbit" almost better than anybody else in the Forest; but there was another animal there nowadays, the strange and Bouncy Tigger; and he was the sort of Tigger who was always in front when you were showing him the way anywhere, and was generally out of sight when at last you came to the place and said proudly "Here we are!"

"No, not Kanga's," said Rabbit thoughtfully to himself, as he curled his whiskers in the sun; and, to make quite sure that he wasn't going there, he turned to the left and trotted off in the other direction, which was the way to Christopher Robin's house.

"After all," said Rabbit to himself, "Christopher Robin depends on Me. He's fond of Pooh and Piglet and Eeyore, and so am I, but they haven't any Brain. Not to notice. And he respects Owl, because you can't help respecting anybody who can spell TUESDAY, even if he doesn't spell it right; but spelling isn't everything. There are days when spelling Tuesday simply doesn't count. And Kanga is too busy looking after Roo, and Roo is too young and Tigger is too bouncy to be of any help, so there's really nobody but

Me, when you come to look at it. I'll go and see if there's anything he wants doing, and then I'll do it for him. It's just the day for doing things."

He trotted along happily, and by-and-by he crossed the stream and came to the place where his friends-and-relations lived. There seemed to be even more of them about than usual this morning, and having nodded to a hedgehog or two, with whom he was too busy to shake hands and having said, "Good morning, good morning," importantly to some of the others, and "Ah, there you are," kindly, to the smaller ones, he waved a paw at them over his shoulder, and was gone; leaving such an air of excitement and I-don't-know-what behind him, that several members of the Beetle family, including Henry Rush, made their way at once to the Hundred Acre Wood and began climbing trees, in the hope of getting to the top before it happened, whatever it was, so that they might see it properly.

Rabbit hurried on by the edge of the Hundred Acre Wood, feeling more important every minute, and soon he came to the tree where Christopher Robin lived. He knocked at the door, and he called out once or twice, and then he walked back a little way and put his paw up to keep the sun out, and called to the top of the tree, and then he turned all round and shouted "Hallo!" and "I say!" "It's Rabbit!" – but nothing happened. Then he stopped and listened, and everything stopped and listened with him, and the Forest was very lone and still and peaceful in the sunshine, until suddenly a hundred miles above him a lark began to sing.

"Bother!" said Rabbit. "He's gone out."

He went back to the green front door, just to make sure, and he was turning away, feeling that his morning had got all spoilt, when he saw a piece

of paper on the ground. And there was a pin in it, as if it had fallen off the door.

"Ha!" said Rabbit, feeling quite happy again. "Another notice!"

This is what it said:

GON OUT
BACKSON
BISY
BACKSON

C.R.

"Ha!" said Rabbit again. "I must tell the others." And he hurried off importantly.

The nearest house was Owl's, and to Owl's House in the Hundred Acre Wood he made his way. He came to Owl's door, and he knocked and he rang, and he rang and he knocked, and at last Owl's head came out and said "Go away, I'm thinking – oh, it's you?" which was how he always began.

"Owl," said Rabbit shortly, "you and I have brains. The others have fluff. If there is any thinking to be done in this Forest – and when I say thinking I mean *thinking* – you and I must do it."

"Yes," said Owl. "I was."

"Read that."

Owl took Christopher Robin's notice from Rabbit and looked at it nervously. He could spell his own name WOL, and he could spell Tuesday so that you knew it wasn't Wednesday, and he could read quite comfortably when you weren't looking over his shoulder and saying "Well?" all the time, and he could —

"Well?" said Rabbit.

"Yes," said Owl, looking Wise and Thoughtful. "I see what you mean. Undoubtedly."

"Well?"

"Exactly," said Owl. "Precisely." And he added, after a little thought, "If you had not come to me, I should have come to you."

"Why?" asked Rabbit.

"For that very reason," said Owl, hoping that something helpful would happen soon.

"Yesterday morning," said Rabbit solemnly, "I went to see Christopher Robin. He was out. Pinned on his door was a notice!"

"The same notice?"

"A different one. But the meaning was the same. It's very odd."

"Amazing," said Owl, looking at the notice again, and getting, just for a moment, a curious sort of feeling that something had happened to Christopher Robin's back. "What did you do?"

"Nothing."

"The best thing," said Owl wisely.

"Well?" said Rabbit again, as Owl knew he was going to.

"Exactly," said Owl.

For a little while he couldn't think of anything more; and then, all of a sudden, he had an idea.

"Tell me, Rabbit," he said, "the *exact* words of the first notice. This is very important. Everything depends on this. The *exact* words of the *first* notice."

"It was just the same as that one really."

Owl looked at him, and wondered whether to push him off the tree; but, feeling that he could always do it afterwards, he tried once more to find out what they were talking about.

"The exact words, please," he said, as if Rabbit hadn't spoken.

"It just said, 'Gon out. Backson.' Same as this, only this says 'Bisy Backson' too."

Owl gave a great sigh of relief.

"Ah!" said Owl. "*Now* we know where we are."

"Yes, but where's Christopher Robin?" said Rabbit. "That's the point."

Owl looked at the notice again. To one of his education the reading of it was easy. "Gon out, Backson. Bisy, Backson" – just the sort of thing you'd expect to see on a notice.

"It is quite clear what has happened, my dear Rabbit," he said. "Christopher Robin has gone out somewhere with Backson. He and Backson are busy together. Have you seen a Backson anywhere about in the Forest lately?"

"I don't know," said Rabbit. "That's what I came to ask you. What are they like?"

"Well," said Owl, "the Spotted or Herbaceous Backson is just a —"

"At least," he said, "It's really more of a —"

"Of course," he said, "it depends on the —"

"Well," said Owl, "the fact is," he said, "I don't know *what* they're like," said Owl frankly.

"Thank you," said Rabbit. And he hurried off to see Pooh.

Before he had gone very far he heard a noise. So he stopped and listened. This was the noise:

NOISE, BY POOH

Oh, the butterflies are flying,
Now the winter days are dying,
And the primroses are trying
 To be seen.
And the turtle-doves are cooing,
And the woods are up and doing,
For the violets are blue-ing
 In the green.

Oh, the honey-bees are gumming
On their little wings, and humming
That the summer, which is coming,
    Will be fun.
And the cows are almost cooing,
And the turtle-doves are mooing,
Which is why a Pooh is poohing
    In the sun.

For the spring is really springing;
You can see a skylark singing,
And the blue-bells, which are ringing,
    Can be heard.
And the cuckoo isn't cooing,
But he's cucking and he's ooing,
And a Pooh is simply poohing
    Like a bird.

"Hallo, Pooh," said Rabbit.

"Hallo, Rabbit," said Pooh dreamily.

"Did you make that song up?"

"Well, I sort of made it up," said Pooh. "It isn't Brain," he went on humbly, "because You Know Why, Rabbit; but it comes to me sometimes."

"Ah!" said Rabbit, who never let things come to him, but always went and fetched them. "Well, the point is, have you seen a Spotted or Herbaceous Backson in the Forest, at all?"

"No," said Pooh. "Not a – no," said Pooh. "I saw Tigger just now."

"That's no good."

"No," said Pooh. "I thought it wasn't."

"Have you seen Piglet?"

"Yes," said Pooh. "I suppose *that* isn't any good either?" he asked meekly.

"Well, it depends if he saw anything."

"He saw me," said Pooh.

Rabbit sat down on the ground next to Pooh, and, feeling much less important like that, stood up again.

"What it all comes to is this," he said. "*What does Christopher Robin do in the morning nowadays?*"

"What sort of thing?"

"Well, can you tell me anything you've seen him do in the morning? These last few days."

"Yes," said Pooh. "We had breakfast together yesterday. By the Pine Trees.

I'd made up a little basket, just a little, fair-sized basket, an ordinary biggish sort of basket, full of —"

"Yes, yes," said Rabbit, "but I mean later than that. Have you seen him between eleven and twelve?"

"Well," said Pooh, "at eleven o'clock – at eleven o'clock – well, at eleven o'clock, you see, I generally get home about then. Because I have One or Two Things to Do."

"Quarter past eleven, then?"

"Well — " said Pooh.

"Half past?"

"Yes," said Pooh. "At half past – or perhaps later – I might see him."

And now that he did think of it, he began to remember that he *hadn't* seen Christopher Robin about so much lately. Not in the mornings. Afternoons, yes; evenings, yes; before breakfast, yes; just after breakfast, yes. And then, perhaps, "See you again, Pooh," and off he'd go.

"That's just it," said Rabbit. "Where?"

"Perhaps he's looking for something."

"What?" asked Rabbit.

"That's just what I was going to say," said Pooh. And then he added, "Perhaps he's looking for a – for a —"

"A Spotted or Herbaceous Backson?"

"Yes," said Pooh. "One of those. In case it isn't."

Rabbit looked at him severely.

"I don't think you're helping," he said.

"No," said Pooh. "I do try," he added humbly.

Rabbit thanked him for trying, and said that he would now go and see Eeyore, and Pooh could walk with him if he liked. But Pooh, who felt another verse of his song coming on him, said he would wait for Piglet, good-bye, Rabbit; so Rabbit went off.

But, as it happened, it was Rabbit who saw Piglet first. Piglet had got up early that morning to pick himself a bunch of violets; and when he had picked them and put them in a pot in the middle of his house, it suddenly came over him that nobody had ever picked Eeyore a bunch of violets, and the more he thought of this, the more he thought how sad it was to be an Animal who had never had a bunch of violets picked for him. So he hurried out again, saying to himself, "Eeyore, Violets," and then "Violets, Eeyore," in case he forgot, because it was that sort of day, and he picked a large bunch and trotted along, smelling them, and feeling very happy, until he came to the place where Eeyore was.

"Oh, Eeyore," began Piglet a little nervously, because Eeyore was busy.
Eeyore put out a paw and waved him away.
"Tomorrow," said Eeyore. "Or the next day."
Piglet came a little closer to see what it was. Eeyore had three sticks on the ground, and was looking at them. Two of the sticks were touching at one end, but not at the other, and the third stick was laid across them. Piglet thought that perhaps it was a Trap of some kind.
"Oh, Eeyore," he began again, "I just —"
"Is that little Piglet?" said Eeyore, still looking hard at his sticks.
"Yes, Eeyore, and I —"
"Do you know what this is?"
"No," said Piglet.
"It's an A."
"Oh," said Piglet.

"Not O – A," said Eeyore severely. "Can't you *hear*, or do you think you have more education than Christopher Robin?"

"Yes," said Piglet. "No," said Piglet very quickly. And he came closer still.

"Christopher Robin said it was an A, and an A it is – until somebody treads on it," Eeyore added sternly.

Piglet jumped backwards hurriedly, and smelt at his violets.

"Do you know what A means, little Piglet?"

"No, Eeyore, I don't."

"It means Learning, it means Education, it means all the things that you and Pooh haven't got. That's what A means."

"Oh," said Piglet again. "I mean, does it?" he explained quickly.

"I'm telling you. People come and go in this Forest, and they say, 'It's only Eeyore, so it doesn't count.' They walk to and fro saying 'Ha ha!' But do they know anything about A? They don't. It's just three sticks to *them*. But to the Educated – mark this, little Piglet – to the Educated, not meaning Poohs and Piglets, it's a great and glorious A. Not," he added, "just something that anybody can come and *breathe* on."

Piglet stepped back nervously, and looked round for help.

"Here's Rabbit," he said gladly. "Hallo, Rabbit."

Rabbit came up importantly, nodded to Piglet, and said, "Ah, Eeyore," in the voice of one who would be saying "Good-bye" in about two more minutes.

"There's just one thing I wanted to ask you, Eeyore. What happens to Christopher Robin in the mornings nowadays?"

"What's this that I'm looking at?" said Eeyore still looking at it.

"Three sticks," said Rabbit promptly.

"You see?" said Eeyore to Piglet. He turned to Rabbit. "I will now answer your question," he said solemnly.

"Thank you," said Rabbit.

"What does Christopher Robin do in the mornings? He learns. He becomes Educated. He instigates – I *think* that is the word he mentioned, but I may be referring to something else – he instigorates Knowledge. In my small way I also, if I have the word right, am – am doing what he does. That, for instance, is —"

"An A," said Rabbit, "but not a very good one. Well, I must get back and tell the others."

Eeyore looked at his sticks and then he looked at Piglet.

"What did Rabbit say it was?" he asked.

"An A," said Piglet.

"Did you tell him?"

"No, Eeyore, I didn't. I expect he just knew."

"He *knew*? You mean this A thing is a thing *Rabbit* knew?"

"Yes, Eeyore. He's clever, Rabbit is."

"Clever!" said Eeyore scornfully, putting a foot heavily on his three sticks. "Education!" said Eeyore bitterly, jumping on his six sticks. "What *is* Learning?" asked Eeyore as he kicked his twelve sticks into the air. "A thing *Rabbit* knows! Ha!"

"I think —" began Piglet nervously.

"Don't," said Eeyore.

"I think *Violets* are rather nice," said Piglet. And he laid his bunch in front of Eeyore and scampered off.

Next morning the notice on Christopher Robin's door said:

GONE OUT
BACK SOON
C.R.

Which is why all the animals in the Forest – except, of course, the Spotted and Herbaceous Backson – now know what Christopher Robin does in the mornings.

US TWO

Wherever I am, there's always Pooh,
There's always Pooh and Me.
Whatever I do, he wants to do,
"Where are you going today?" says Pooh:
"Well, that's very odd 'cos I was too.
Let's go together," says Pooh, says he.
"Let's go together," says Pooh.

"What's twice eleven?" I said to Pooh,
("Twice what?" said Pooh to Me.)
"I *think* it ought to be twenty-two."
"Just what I think myself," said Pooh.
"It wasn't an easy sum to do,
But that's what it is," said Pooh, said
"That's what it is," said Pooh.

"Let's look for dragons," I said to Pooh.
"Yes, let's," said Pooh to Me.
We crossed the river and found a few –
"Yes, those are dragons all right," said Pooh.
"As soon as I saw their beaks I knew.
That's what they are," said Pooh, said he.
"That's what they are," said Pooh.

"Let's frighten the dragons," I said to Pooh.
"That's right," said Pooh to Me.
"*I'm* not afraid," I said to Pooh,
And I held his paw and I shouted, "Shoo!
Silly old dragons!" – and off they flew.
"I wasn't afraid," said Pooh, said he,
"I'm *never* afraid with you."

So wherever I am, there's always Pooh,
There's always Pooh and Me.
"What would I do?" I said to Pooh,
"If it wasn't for you," and Pooh said: "True,
It isn't much fun for One, but Two
Can stick together," says Pooh, says he.
"That's how it is," says Pooh.

KNIGHT IN ARMOUR

Whenever I'm a shining Knight,
I buckle on my armour tight;
And then I look about for things,
Like Rushings-out, and Rescuings,
And Savings from the Dragon's Lair,
And fighting all the Dragons there.
And sometimes when our fights begin,
I think I'll let the Dragons win . . .
And then I think perhaps I won't,
Because they're Dragons, and I don't.

Pooh Invents a New Game

By the time it came to the edge of the Forest the stream had grown up, so that it was almost a river, and, being grown-up, it did not run and jump and sparkle along as it used to do when it was younger, but moved more slowly. For it knew now where it was going, and it said to itself, "There is no hurry. We shall get there some day." But all the little streams higher up in the Forest went this way and that, quickly, eagerly, having so much to find out before it was too late.

There was a broad track, almost as broad as a road, leading from the Outland to the Forest, but before it could come to the Forest, it had to cross this river. So, where it crossed, there was a wooden bridge, almost as broad as a road, with wooden rails on each side of it. Christopher Robin could just get his chin on to the top rail, if he wanted to, but it was more fun to stand on the bottom rail, so that he could lean right over, and watch the river slipping slowly away beneath him. Pooh could get his chin on to the bottom rail if he wanted to, but it was more fun to lie down and get his head under it, and watch the river slipping slowly away beneath him. And this was the only way in which Piglet and Roo could watch the river at all, because they were too small to reach the bottom rail. So they would lie down and watch it . . . and it slipped away very slowly, being in no hurry to get there.

One day, when Pooh was walking towards this bridge, he was trying to make up a piece of poetry about fir-cones, because there they were, lying about on each side of him, and he felt singy. So he picked a fir-cone up, and looked at it, and said to himself, "This is a very good fir-cone, and something ought to rhyme to it." But he couldn't think of anything. And then this came into his head suddenly:

Here is a myst'ry
About a little fir-tree.
Owl says it's *his* tree,
And Kanga says it's *her* tree.

"Which doesn't make sense," said Pooh, "because Kanga doesn't live in a tree."

He had just come to the bridge; and not looking where he was going, he tripped over something, and the fir-cone jerked out of his paw into the river.

"Bother," said Pooh, as it floated slowly under the bridge, and he went back to get another fir-cone which had a rhyme to it. But then he thought that he would just look at the river instead, because it was a peaceful sort of day, so he lay down and looked at it, and it slipped slowly away beneath him . . . and suddenly, there was his fir-cone slipping away too.

"That's funny," said Pooh. "I dropped it on the other side," said Pooh, "and it came out on this side! I wonder if it would do it again?" And he went back for some more fir-cones.

It did. It kept on doing it. Then he dropped two in at once, and leant over the bridge to see which of them would come out first; and one of them did; but as they were both the same size, he didn't know if it was the one which he wanted to win, or the other one. So the next time he dropped one big one and one little one, and the big one came out first, which was what he had said it would do, and the little one came out last, which was what he had said it would do, so he had won twice . . . and when he went home for tea, he had won thirty-six and lost twenty-eight, which meant that he was – that he had – well, you take twenty-eight from thirty-six, and *that's* what he was. Instead of the other way round.

And that was the beginning of the game called Poohsticks, which Pooh invented, and which he and his friends used to play on the edge of the Forest. But they played with sticks instead of fir-cones, because they were easier to mark.

Now one day Pooh and Piglet and Rabbit and Roo were all playing

Poohsticks together. They had dropped their sticks in when Rabbit said "Go!" and then they had hurried across to the other side of the bridge, and now they were all leaning over the edge, waiting to see whose stick would come out first. But it was a long time coming, because the river was very lazy that day, and hardly seemed to mind if it didn't ever get there at all.

"I can see mine!" cried Roo. "No, I can't, it's something else. Can you see yours, Piglet? I thought I could see mine, but I couldn't. There it is! No, it isn't. Can you see yours, Pooh?"

"No," said Pooh.

"I expect my stick's stuck," said Roo. "Rabbit, my stick's stuck. Is your stick stuck, Piglet?"

"They always take longer than you think," said Rabbit.

"How long do you *think* they'll take?" asked Roo.

"I can see yours, Piglet," said Pooh suddenly.

"Mine's a sort of greyish one," said Piglet, not daring to lean too far over in case he fell in.

"Yes, that's what I can see. It's coming over on to my side."

Rabbit leant over further than ever, looking for his, and Roo wriggled up and down, calling out "Come on, stick! Stick, stick, stick!" and Piglet got very excited because his was the only one which had been seen, and that meant that he was winning.

"It's coming!" said Pooh.

"Are you *sure* it's mine?" squeaked Piglet excitedly.

"Yes, because it's grey. A big grey one. Here it comes!
A very – big – grey — Oh, no, it isn't, it's Eeyore."

And out floated Eeyore.

"Eeyore!" cried everybody.

Looking very calm, very dignified, with his legs in the air, came Eeyore from beneath the bridge.

"It's Eeyore!" cried Roo, terribly excited.

"Is that so?" said Eeyore, getting caught up by a little eddy, and turning slowly round three times. "I wondered."

"I didn't know you were playing," said Roo.

"I'm not," said Eeyore.

"Eeyore, what *are* you doing there?" said Rabbit.

"I'll give you three guesses, Rabbit. Digging holes in the ground? Wrong.

Leaping from branch to branch of a young oak-tree? Wrong. Waiting for somebody to help me out of the river? Right. Give Rabbit time, and he'll always get the answer."

"But, Eeyore," said Pooh in distress, "what can we – I mean, how shall we – do you think if we —"

"Yes," said Eeyore. "One of those would be just the thing. Thank you, Pooh."

"He's going *round* and *round*," said Roo, much impressed.

"And why not?" said Eeyore coldly.

"I can swim too," said Roo proudly.

"Not round and round," said Eeyore. "It's much more difficult. I didn't want to come swimming at all today," he went on, revolving slowly. "But if, when in, I decide to practise a slight circular movement from right to left – or perhaps I should say," he added, as he got into another eddy, "from left to right, just as it happens to occur to me, it is nobody's business but my own."

There was a moment's silence while everybody thought.

"I've got a sort of idea," said Pooh at last, "but I don't suppose it's a very good one."

"I don't suppose it is either," said Eeyore.

"Go on, Pooh," said Rabbit. "Let's have it."

"Well, if we all threw stones and things into the river on *one* side of Eeyore, the stones would make waves, and the waves would wash him to the other side."

"That's a very good idea," said Rabbit, and Pooh looked happy again.

"Very," said Eeyore. "When I want to be washed, Pooh, I'll let you know."

"Supposing we hit him by mistake?" said Piglet anxiously.

"Or supposing you missed him by mistake," said Eeyore. "Think of all the possibilities, Piglet, before you settle down to enjoy yourselves."

But Pooh had got the biggest stone he could carry, and was leaning over the bridge, holding it in his paws.

"I'm not throwing it, I'm dropping it, Eeyore," he explained. "And then I can't miss – I mean I can't hit you. *Could* you stop turning round for a moment, because it muddles me rather?"

"No," said Eeyore. "I *like* turning round."

Rabbit began to feel that it was time he took command.

"Now, Pooh," he said, "when I say 'Now!' you can drop it. Eeyore, when I say 'Now!' Pooh will drop his stone."

"Thank you very much, Rabbit, but I expect I shall know."

"Are you ready, Pooh? Piglet, give Pooh a little more room. Get back a bit there, Roo. Are you ready?"

"No," said Eeyore.

"*Now!*" said Rabbit.

Pooh dropped his stone. There was a loud splash, and Eeyore disappeared. . . .

It was an anxious moment for the watchers on the bridge. They looked and looked . . . and even the sight of Piglet's stick coming out a little in front of Rabbit's didn't cheer them up as much as you would have expected. And then, just as Pooh was beginning to think that he must have chosen the wrong stone or the wrong river or the wrong day for his Idea, something grey showed for a moment by the river bank . . . and it got slowly bigger and bigger . . . and at last it was Eeyore coming out.

With a shout they rushed off the bridge, and pushed and pulled at him; and soon he was standing among them again on dry land.

"Oh, Eeyore, you *are* wet!" said Piglet, feeling him.

Eeyore shook himself, and asked somebody to explain to Piglet what happened when you had been inside a river for quite a long time.

"Well done, Pooh," said Rabbit kindly. "That was a good idea of ours."

"What was?" asked Eeyore.

"Hooshing you to the bank like that."

"*Hooshing* me?" said Eeyore in surprise. "Hooshing *me?* You didn't think I was *hooshed*, did you? I dived. Pooh dropped a large stone on me, and so as not to be struck heavily on the chest, I dived and swam to the bank."

"You didn't really," whispered Piglet to Pooh, so as to comfort him.

"I didn't *think* I did," said Pooh anxiously.

"It's just Eeyore," said Piglet. "*I* thought your Idea was a very good Idea."

Pooh began to feel a little more comfortable, because when you are a Bear of Very Little Brain, and you Think of Things, you find sometimes that a Thing which seemed very Thingish inside you is quite different when it gets out into the open and has other people looking at it. And, anyhow, Eeyore *was* in the river, and now he *wasn't*, so he hadn't done any harm.

"How did you fall in, Eeyore?" asked Rabbit, as he dried him with Piglet's handkerchief.

"I didn't," said Eeyore.

"But how —"

"I was BOUNCED," said Eeyore.

"Oo," said Roo excitedly, "did somebody push you?"

"Somebody BOUNCED me. I was just thinking by the side of the river – thinking, if any of you know what that means – when I received a loud BOUNCE."

"Oh, Eeyore!" said everybody.

"Are you sure you didn't slip?" asked Rabbit wisely.

"Of course I slipped. If you're standing on the slippery bank of a river, and somebody BOUNCES you loudly from behind, you slip. What did you think I did?"

"But who did it?" asked Roo.

Eeyore didn't answer.

"I expect it was Tigger," said Piglet nervously.

"But, Eeyore," said Pooh, "was it a Joke, or an Accident? I mean —"

"I didn't stop to ask, Pooh. Even at the very bottom of the river I didn't stop to say to myself, '*Is* this a Hearty Joke, or is it the Merest Accident?' I just floated to the surface, and said to myself, 'It's wet.' If you know what I mean."

"And where was Tigger?" asked Rabbit.

Before Eeyore could answer, there was a loud noise behind them, and through the hedge came Tigger himself.

"Hallo, everybody," said Tigger cheerfully.

"Hallo, Tigger," said Roo.

Rabbit became very important suddenly.

"Tigger," he said solemnly, "what happened just now?"

"Just when?" said Tigger a little uncomfortably.

"When you bounced Eeyore into the river."

"I didn't bounce him."

"You bounced me," said Eeyore gruffly.

"I didn't really. I had a cough, and I happened to be behind Eeyore, and I said '*Grrrr-oppp-ptschschschz.*'"

"Why?" said Rabbit, helping Piglet up, and dusting him. "It's all right, Piglet."

"It took me by surprise," said Piglet nervously.

"That's what I call bouncing," said Eeyore. "Taking people by surprise. Very unpleasant habit. I don't mind Tigger being in the Forest," he went on, "because it's a large Forest, and there's plenty of room to bounce in it. But I don't see why he should come into *my* little corner of it, and bounce there. It isn't as if there was anything very wonderful about my little corner. Of course for people who like cold, wet, ugly bits it *is* something rather special, but otherwise it's just a corner, and if anybody feels bouncy —"

"I didn't bounce, I coughed," said Tigger crossly.

"Bouncy or coffy, it's all the same at the bottom of the river."

"Well," said Rabbit, "all I can say is – well, here's Christopher Robin, so *he* can say it."

Christopher Robin came down from the Forest to the bridge, feeling all sunny and careless, and just as if twice nineteen didn't matter a bit, as it didn't on such a happy afternoon, and he thought that if he stood on the bottom rail of the bridge, and leant over, and watched the river slipping slowly away beneath him, then he would suddenly know everything that there was to be known, and he would be able to tell Pooh, who wasn't quite sure about some of it. But when he got to the bridge and saw all the animals there, then he knew that it wasn't that kind of afternoon, but the other kind, when you wanted to *do* something.

"It's like this, Christopher Robin," began Rabbit. "Tigger —"

"No, I didn't," said Tigger.

"Well, anyhow, there I was," said Eeyore.

"But I don't think he meant to," said Pooh.

"He just *is* bouncy," said Piglet, "and he can't help it."

"Try bouncing *me*, Tigger," said Roo eagerly. "Eeyore, Tigger's going to try *me*. Piglet, do you think—"

"Yes, yes," said Rabbit, "we don't all want to speak at once. The point is, what does Christopher Robin think about it?"

"All I did was I coughed," said Tigger.

"He bounced," said Eeyore.

"Well, I sort of boffed," said Tigger.

"Hush!" said Rabbit, holding up his paw. "What does Christopher Robin think about it all? That's the point."

"Well," said Christopher Robin, not quite sure what it was all about. "I think —"

"Yes?" said everybody.

"I think we all ought to play Poohsticks."

So they did. And Eeyore, who had never played it before, won more times than anybody else; and Roo fell in twice, the first time by accident and the second time on purpose, because he suddenly saw Kanga coming from the Forest, and he knew he'd have to go to bed anyhow. So then Rabbit said he'd go with them; and Tigger and Eeyore went off together, because Eeyore wanted to tell Tigger How to Win at Poohsticks, which you do by letting your stick drop in a twitchy sort of way, if you understand what I mean, Tigger; and Christopher Robin and Pooh and Piglet were left on the bridge by themselves.

For a long time they looked at the river beneath them, saying nothing, and the river said nothing too, for it felt very quiet and peaceful on this summer afternoon.

"Tigger is all right, *really*," said Piglet lazily.

"Of course he is," said Christopher Robin.

"Everybody is *really*," said Pooh. "That's what *I* think," said Pooh. "But I don't suppose I'm right," he said.

"Of course you are," said Christopher Robin.

THE ENGINEER

Let it rain!
Who cares?
I've a train
Upstairs,
With a brake
Which I make
From a string
Sort of thing,
Which works
In jerks,
'Cos it drops
In the spring,
Which stops
With the string,

And the wheels
All stick
So quick
That it feels
Like a thing
That you make
With a brake,
Not string. . . .

So that's what I make,
When the day's all wet.
It's a good sort of brake
But it hasn't worked yet.

Tigger is Unbounced

One day Rabbit and Piglet were sitting outside Pooh's front door listening to Rabbit, and Pooh was sitting with them. It was a drowsy summer afternoon, and the Forest was full of gentle sounds, which all seemed to be saying to Pooh, "Don't listen to Rabbit, listen to me." So he got into a comfortable position for not listening to Rabbit, and from time to time he opened his eyes to say "Ah!" and then closed them again to say "True," and from time to time Rabbit said, "You see what I mean, Piglet," very earnestly, and Piglet nodded earnestly to show that he did.

"In fact," said Rabbit, coming to the end of it at last, "Tigger's getting so Bouncy nowadays that it's time we taught him a lesson. Don't you think so, Piglet?"

Piglet said that Tigger *was* very Bouncy, and that if they could think of a way of unbouncing him it would be a Very Good Idea.

"Just what I feel," said Rabbit. "What do *you* say, Pooh?"

Pooh opened his eyes with a jerk and said, "Extremely."

"Extremely what?" asked Rabbit.

"What you were saying," said Pooh. "Undoubtably."

Piglet gave Pooh a stiffening sort of nudge, and Pooh, who felt more and more that he was somewhere else, got up slowly and began to look for himself.

"But how shall we do it?" asked Piglet. "What sort of a lesson, Rabbit?"

"That's the point," said Rabbit.

The word "lesson" came back to Pooh as one he had heard before somewhere.

"There's a thing called Twy-stymes," he said. "Christopher Robin tried to teach it to me once, but it didn't."

"What didn't?" said Rabbit.

"Didn't what?" said Piglet.

Pooh shook his head.

"I don't know," he said. "It just didn't. What are we talking about?"

"Pooh," said Piglet reproachfully, "haven't you been listening to what Rabbit was saying?"

"I listened, but I had a small piece of fluff in my ear. Could you say it again, please, Rabbit?"

Rabbit never minded saying things again, so he asked where he should begin from; and when Pooh had said from the moment when the fluff got in his ear, and Rabbit had asked when that was, and Pooh had said he didn't know because he hadn't heard properly, Piglet settled it all by saying that what they were trying to do was, they were just trying to think of a way to get the bounces out of Tigger, because however much you liked him, you couldn't deny it, he *did* bounce.

"Oh, I see," said Pooh.

"There's too much of him," said Rabbit, "that's what it comes to."

Pooh tried to think, and all he could think of was something which didn't help at all. So he hummed it very quietly to himself.

If Rabbit
Was bigger
And fatter
And stronger,
Or bigger
Than Tigger,
If Tigger was smaller,
Then Tigger's bad habit
Of bouncing at Rabbit
Would matter
No longer,
If Rabbit
Was taller.

"What was Pooh saying?" asked Rabbit. "Any good?"

"No," said Pooh sadly. "No good."

"Well, I've got an idea," said Rabbit, "and here it is. We take Tigger for a long explore, somewhere where he's never been, and we lose him there, and next morning we find him again, and – mark my words – he'll be a different Tigger altogether."

"Why?" said Pooh.

"Because he'll be a Humble Tigger. Because he'll be a Sad Tigger, a Melancholy Tigger, a Small and Sorry Tigger, an Oh-Rabbit-I-*am*-glad-to-see-you Tigger. That's why."

"Will he be glad to see me and Piglet, too?"

"Of course."

"That's good," said Pooh.

"I should hate him to go *on* being Sad," said Piglet doubtfully.

"Tiggers never go on being Sad," explained Rabbit. "They get over it with Astonishing Rapidity. I asked Owl, just to make sure, and he said that that's what they always get over it with. But if we can make Tigger feel Small and

Sad just for five minutes, we shall have done a good deed."

"Would Christopher Robin think so?" asked Piglet.

"Yes," said Rabbit. "He'd say 'You've done a good deed, Piglet. I would have done it myself, only I happened to be doing something else. Thank you, Piglet.' And Pooh, of course."

Piglet felt very glad about this, and he saw at once that what they were going to do to Tigger was a good thing to do, and as Pooh and Rabbit were doing it with him, it was a thing which even a Very Small Animal could wake up in the morning and be comfortable about doing. So the only question was, where should they lose Tigger?

"We'll take him to the North Pole," said Rabbit, "because it was a very long explore finding it, so it will be a very long explore for Tigger un-finding it again."

It was now Pooh's turn to feel very glad, because it was he who had first found the North Pole, and when they got there, Tigger would see a notice which said, "Discovered by Pooh, Pooh found it," and then Tigger would know, which perhaps he didn't now, the sort of Bear Pooh was. *That* sort of Bear.

So it was arranged that they should start next morning, and that Rabbit, who lived near Kanga and Roo and Tigger, should now go home and ask Tigger what he was doing tomorrow, because if he wasn't doing anything, what about coming for an explore and getting Pooh and Piglet to come too? And if Tigger said "Yes" that would be all right, and if he said "No" —

"He won't," said Rabbit. "Leave it to me." And he went off busily.

The next day was quite a different day. Instead of being hot and sunny, it was cold and misty. Pooh didn't mind for himself, but when he thought of all the honey the bees wouldn't be making, a cold and misty day always made him feel sorry for them. He said so to Piglet when Piglet came to fetch him, and Piglet said that he wasn't thinking of that so much, but of how cold and miserable it would be being lost all day and night on the top of the Forest. But when he and Pooh had got to Rabbit's house, Rabbit said it was just the day for them, because Tigger always bounced on ahead of everybody, and as soon as he got out of sight, they would hurry away in the other direction, and he would never see them again.

"Not never?" said Piglet.

"Well, not until we find him again, Piglet. Tomorrow, or whenever it is. Come on. He's waiting for us."

When they got to Kanga's house, they found that Roo was waiting too, being a great friend of Tigger's, which made it Awkward; but Rabbit whispered "Leave this to me" behind his paw to Pooh, and went up to Kanga.

"I don't think Roo had better come," he said. "Not today."

"Why not?" said Roo, who wasn't supposed to be listening.

"Nasty cold day," said Rabbit, shaking his head. "And you were coughing this morning."

"How do you know?" asked Roo indignantly.

"Oh, Roo, you never told me," said Kanga reproachfully.

"It was a biscuit cough," said Roo, "not one you tell about."

"I think not today, dear. Another day."

"Tomorrow?" said Roo hopefully.

"We'll see," said Kanga.

"You're always seeing, and nothing ever happens," said Roo sadly.

"Nobody could see on a day like this, Roo," said Rabbit. "I don't expect we shall get very far, and then this afternoon we'll all – we'll all – we'll – ah, Tigger, there you are. Come on. Good-bye, Roo! This afternoon we'll – come on, Pooh! All ready? That's right. Come on."

So they went. At first Pooh and Rabbit and
Piglet walked together, and Tigger ran round them
in circles, and then, when the path got narrower,
Rabbit, Piglet and Pooh walked one after another,
and Tigger ran round them in oblongs, and by-
and-by, when the gorse got very prickly on each
side of the path, Tigger ran up and down in front
of them, and sometimes he bounced into Rabbit
and sometimes he didn't. And as they got higher,
the mist got thicker, so that Tigger kept
disappearing, and then when you thought he wasn't there, there he was again,
saying, "I say, come on," and before you could say anything, there he wasn't.

Rabbit turned round and nudged Piglet.

"The next time," he said. "Tell Pooh."

"The next time," said Piglet to Pooh.

"The next what?" said Pooh to Piglet.

Tigger appeared suddenly, bounced into Rabbit, and disappeared again.
"Now!" said Rabbit. He jumped into a hollow by the side of the path, and
Pooh and Piglet jumped after him. They crouched in the bracken, listening.
The Forest was very silent when you stopped and listened to it. They could
see nothing and hear nothing.

"H'sh!" said Rabbit.

"I am," said Pooh.

There was a pattering noise . . . then silence again.

"Hallo!" said Tigger, and he sounded so close suddenly that Piglet would have jumped if Pooh hadn't accidentally been sitting on most of him.

"Where are you?" called Tigger.

Rabbit nudged Pooh, and Pooh looked about for Piglet to nudge, but couldn't find him, and Piglet went on breathing wet bracken as quietly as he could, and felt very brave and excited.

."That's funny," said Tigger.

There was a moment's silence, and then they heard him pattering off again. For a little longer they waited, until the Forest had become so still that it almost frightened them, and then Rabbit got up and stretched himself.

"Well?" he whispered proudly. "There we are! Just as I said."

"I've been thinking," said Pooh, "and I think —"

"No," said Rabbit. "Don't. Run. Come on." And they all hurried off, Rabbit leading the way.

"Now," said Rabbit, after they had gone a little way, "we can talk. What were you going to say, Pooh?"

"Nothing much. Why are we going along here?"

"Because it's the way home."

"Oh!" said Pooh.

"I *think* it's more to the right," said Piglet nervously. "What do *you* think, Pooh?"

Pooh looked at his two paws. He knew that one of them was the right, and he knew that when you had decided which one of them was the right, then the other one was the left, but he never could remember how to begin.

"Well —" he said slowly.

"Come on," said Rabbit. "I know it's this way."

They went on. Ten minutes later they stopped again.

"It's very silly," said Rabbit, "but just for the moment I — Ah, of course. Come on." . . .

"Here we are," said Rabbit ten minutes later. "No, we're not.". . .

"Now," said Rabbit ten minutes later, "I think we ought to be getting – or are we a little bit more to the right than I thought?" . . .

"It's a funny thing," said Rabbit ten minutes later, "how everything looks the same in a mist. Have you noticed it, Pooh?"

Pooh said that he had.

"Lucky we know the Forest so well, or we might get lost," said Rabbit half an hour later, and he gave the careless laugh which you give when you know the Forest so well that you can't get lost.

Piglet sidled up to Pooh from behind.

"Pooh!" he whispered.

"Yes, Piglet?"

"Nothing," said Piglet, taking Pooh's paw. "I just wanted to be sure of you."

When Tigger had finished waiting for the others to catch him up, and they hadn't, and when he had got tired of having nobody to say, "I say, come on" to, he thought he would go home. So he trotted back; and the first thing Kanga said when she saw him was, "There's a good Tigger. You're just in time for your Strengthening Medicine," and she poured it out for him. Roo said proudly, "I've *had* mine," and Tigger swallowed his and said, "So have I," and then he and Roo pushed each other about in a friendly way, and Tigger accidentally knocked over one or two chairs by accident, and Roo accidentally knocked over one on purpose, and Kanga said, "Now then, run along."

"Where shall we run along to?" asked Roo.

"You can go and collect some fir-cones for me," said Kanga, giving them a basket.

So they went to the Six Pine Trees, and threw fir-cones at each other until they had forgotten what they came for, and they left the basket under the trees and went back to dinner. And it was just as they were finishing dinner that Christopher Robin put his head in at the door.

"Where's Pooh?" he asked.

"Tigger dear, where's Pooh?" said Kanga. Tigger explained what had happened at the same time that Roo was explaining about his Biscuit Cough and Kanga was telling them not both to talk at once, so it was some time before Christopher Robin guessed that Pooh and Piglet and Rabbit were all lost in the mist on the top of the Forest.

"It's a funny thing about Tiggers," whispered Tigger to Roo, "how Tiggers *never* get lost."

"Why don't they, Tigger?"

"They just don't," explained Tigger. "That's how it is."

"Well," said Christopher Robin, "we shall have to go and find them, that's all. Come on, Tigger."

"I shall have to go and find them," explained Tigger to Roo.

"May I find them too?" asked Roo eagerly.

"I think not today, dear," said Kanga. "Another day."

"Well, if they're lost tomorrow, may I find them?"

"We'll see," said Kanga, and Roo, who knew what *that* meant, went into a corner and practised jumping out at himself, partly because he wanted to practise this, and partly because he didn't want Christopher Robin and Tigger to think that he minded when they went off without him.

"The fact is," said Rabbit, "we've missed our way somehow."

They were having a rest in a small sand-pit on the top of the Forest. Pooh was getting rather tired of that sand-pit, and suspected it of following them about, because whichever direction they started in, they always ended up at it, and each time, as it came through the mist at them, Rabbit said triumphantly, "Now I know where we are!" and Pooh said sadly, "So do I," and Piglet said nothing. He had tried to think of something to say, but the only thing he could think of was, "Help, help!" and it seemed silly to say that, when he had Pooh and Rabbit with him.

"Well," said Rabbit, after a long silence in which nobody thanked him for the nice walk they were having, "we'd better get on, I suppose. Which way shall we try?"

"How would it be," said Pooh slowly, "if, as soon as we're out of sight of this Pit, we try to find it again?"

"What's the good of that?" said Rabbit.

"Well," said Pooh, "we keep looking for Home and not finding it, so I thought that if we looked for this Pit, we'd be sure not to find it, which would be a Good Thing, because then we might find something that we *weren't* looking for, which might be just what we *were* looking for, really."

"I don't see much sense in that," said Rabbit.

"No," said Pooh humbly, "there isn't. But there was *going* to be when I began it. It's just that something happened to it on the way."

"If I walked away from this Pit, and then walked back to it, of *course* I should find it."

"Well, I thought perhaps you wouldn't," said Pooh. "I just thought."

"Try," said Piglet suddenly. "We'll wait here for you."

Rabbit gave a laugh to show how silly Piglet was, and walked into the mist. After he had gone a hundred yards, he turned and walked back again . . . and after Pooh and Piglet had waited twenty minutes for him, Pooh got up.

"I just thought," said Pooh. "Now then, Piglet, let's go home."

"But, Pooh," cried Piglet, all excited, "do you know the way?"

"No," said Pooh. "But there are twelve pots of honey in my cupboard, and they've been calling to me for hours. I couldn't hear them properly before because Rabbit *would* talk, but if nobody says anything except those twelve pots, I *think*, Piglet, I shall know where they're coming from. Come on."

They walked off together; and for a long time Piglet said nothing, so as not to interrupt the pots; and then suddenly he made a squeaky noise . . . and an oo-noise . . . because now he began to know where he was; but he still didn't dare to say so out loud, in case he wasn't. And just when he was getting so sure of himself that it didn't matter whether the pots went on calling or not, there was a shout from in front of them, and out of the mist came Christopher Robin.

"Oh, there you are," said Christopher Robin carelessly, trying to pretend that he hadn't been Anxious.

"Here we are," said Pooh.

"Where's Rabbit?"

"I don't know," said Pooh.

"Oh – well, I expect Tigger will find him. He's sort of looking for you all."

"Well," said Pooh, "I've got to go home for something, and so has Piglet, because we haven't had it yet, and —"

"I'll come and watch you," said Christopher Robin.

So he went home with Pooh, and watched him for quite a long time . . . and all the time he was watching, Tigger was tearing round the Forest making loud yapping noises for Rabbit. And at last a very Small and Sorry Rabbit heard him. And the Small and Sorry Rabbit rushed through the mist at the noise, and it suddenly turned into Tigger; a Friendly Tigger, a Grand Tigger, a Large and Helpful Tigger, a Tigger who bounced, if he bounced at all, in just the beautiful way a Tigger ought to bounce.

"Oh, Tigger, I *am* glad to see you," cried Rabbit.

SPRING MORNING

Where am I going? I don't quite know.
Down to the stream where the king-cups grow –
Up to the hill where the pine-trees blow –
Anywhere, anywhere. *I* don't know.

Where am I going? The clouds sail by,
Little ones, baby ones, over the sky.
Where am I going? The shadows pass,
Little ones, baby ones, over the grass.

If you were a cloud, and sailed up there,
You'd sail on water as blue as air,
And you'd see me here in the fields and say:
"Doesn't the sky look green today?"

Where am I going? The high rooks call:
"It's awful fun to be born at all."
Where am I going? The ring-doves coo:
"We do have beautiful things to do."

If you were a bird, and lived on high,
You'd lean on the wind when the wind came by,
You'd say to the wind when it took you away:
"*That's* where I wanted to go today!"

Where am I going? I don't quite know.
What does it matter where people go?
Down to the wood where the blue-bells grow –
Anywhere, anywhere. *I* don't know.

PIGLET DOES A VERY GRAND THING

Half-way between Pooh's house and Piglet's house was a Thoughtful Spot where they met sometimes when they had decided to go and see each other, and as it was warm and out of the wind they would sit down there for a little and wonder what they would do now that they *had* seen each other. One day when they had decided not to do anything, Pooh made up a verse about it, so that everybody should know what the place was for.

> This warm and sunny Spot
>   Belongs to Pooh.
> And here he wonders what
>   He's going to do.
> Oh, bother, I forgot –
>   It's Piglet's too.

Now one autumn morning when the wind had blown all the leaves off the trees in the night, and was trying to blow the branches off, Pooh and Piglet were sitting in the Thoughtful Spot and wondering.

"What *I* think," said Pooh, "is I think we'll go to Pooh Corner and see Eeyore, because perhaps his house has been blown down, and perhaps he'd like us to build it again."

"What *I* think," said Piglet, "is I think we'll go and see Christopher Robin, only he won't be there, so we can't."

"Let's go and see *everybody*," said Pooh. "Because when you've been walking in the wind for miles, and you suddenly go into somebody's house, and he says, 'Hallo, Pooh, you're just in time for a little smackerel of something,' and you are, then it's what I call a Friendly Day."

Piglet thought that they ought to have a Reason for going to see everybody, like Looking for Small or Organizing an Expotition, if Pooh could think of something.

Pooh could.

"We'll go because it's Thursday," he said, "and we'll go to wish everybody a Very Happy Thursday. Come on, Piglet."

They got up; and when Piglet had sat down again, because he didn't know the wind was so strong, and had been helped up by Pooh, they started off. They went to Pooh's house first, and luckily Pooh was at home just as

they got there, so he asked them in, and they had some, and then they went on to Kanga's house, holding on to each other, and shouting, "Isn't it?" and "What?" and "I can't hear." By the time they got to Kanga's house they were so buffeted that they stayed to lunch. Just at first it seemed rather cold outside afterwards, so they pushed on to Rabbit's as quickly as they could.

"We've come to wish you a Very Happy Thursday," said Pooh, when he had gone in and out once or twice just to make sure that he *could* get out again.

"Why, what's going to happen on Thursday?" asked Rabbit, and when Pooh had explained, and Rabbit, whose life was made up of Important Things, said, "Oh, I thought you'd really come about something," they sat down for a little . . . and by-and-by Pooh and Piglet went on again. The wind was behind them now, so they didn't have to shout.

"Rabbit's clever," said Pooh thoughtfully.

"Yes," said Piglet, "Rabbit's clever."

"And he has Brain."

"Yes," said Piglet, "Rabbit has Brain."

There was a long silence.

"I suppose," said Pooh, "that that's why he never understands anything."

Christopher Robin was at home by this time, because it was the afternoon, and he was so glad to see them that they stayed there until very nearly tea-time, and then they had a Very Nearly tea, which is one you forget about afterwards, and hurried on to Pooh Corner, so as to see Eeyore before it was too late to have a Proper Tea with Owl.

"Hallo, Eeyore," they called out cheerfully.

"Ah!" said Eeyore. "Lost your way?"

"We just came to see you," said Piglet. "And to see how your house was. Look, Pooh, it's still standing!"

"I know," said Eeyore. "Very odd. Somebody ought to have come down and pushed it over."

"We wondered whether the wind would blow it down," said Pooh.

"Ah, that's why nobody's bothered, I suppose. I thought perhaps they'd forgotten."

"Well, we're very glad to see you, Eeyore, and now we're going on to see Owl."

"That's right. You'll like Owl. He flew past a day or two ago and noticed me. He didn't actually say anything, mind you, but he knew it was me. Very friendly of him, I thought. Encouraging."

Pooh and Piglet shuffled about a little and said, "Well, good-bye, Eeyore," as lingeringly as they could, but they had a long way to go, and wanted to be getting on.

"Good-bye," said Eeyore. "Mind you don't get blown away, little Piglet. You'd be missed. People would say, 'Where's little Piglet been blown to?' – really wanting to know. Well, good-bye. And thank you for happening to pass me."

"Good-bye," said Pooh and Piglet for the last time, and they pushed on to Owl's house.

The wind was against them now, and Piglet's ears

 streamed behind him

 like banners

as he fought his way along,

and it seemed hours before he got them into the shelter of the Hundred Acre Wood and they stood up straight again, to listen, a little nervously, to the roaring of the gale among the tree-tops.

"Supposing a tree fell down, Pooh, when we were underneath it?"

"Supposing it didn't," said Pooh after careful thought.

Piglet was comforted by this, and in a little while they were knocking and ringing very cheerfully at Owl's door.

"Hallo, Owl," said Pooh. "I hope we're not too late for – I mean, how are you, Owl? Piglet and I just came to see how you were because it's Thursday."

"Sit down, Pooh, sit down, Piglet," said Owl kindly. "Make yourselves comfortable."

They thanked him, and made themselves as comfortable as they could.

"Because, you see, Owl," said Pooh, "we've been hurrying, so as to be in time for – so as to see you before we went away again."

Owl nodded solemnly.

"Correct me if I am wrong," he said, "but am I right in supposing that it is a very Blusterous day outside?"

"Very," said Piglet, who was quietly thawing his ears, and wishing that he was safely back in his own house. "I thought so," said Owl. "It was on just such a blusterous day as this that my Uncle Robert, a portrait of whom you see upon the wall on your right, Piglet, while returning in the late forenoon from a — What's that?"

There was a loud cracking noise.

"Look out!" cried Pooh. "Mind the clock! Out of the way, Piglet! Piglet, I'm falling on you!"

"Help!" cried Piglet.

Pooh's side of the room was slowly tilting upwards and his chair began sliding down on Piglet's. The clock slithered gently along the mantelpiece, collecting vases on the way, until they all crashed together on to what had once been the floor, but was now trying to see what it looked like as a wall.

Uncle Robert, who was going to be the new hearthrug, and was bringing the rest of his wall with him as carpet, met Piglet's chair just as Piglet was expecting to leave it, and for a little while it became very difficult to remember which was really the north. Then there was another loud crack . . . Owl's room collected itself feverishly . . . and there was silence.

In a corner of the room, the table-cloth began to wriggle.

Then it wrapped itself into a ball and rolled

across the room.

Then it jumped up and down

once or twice, and put out two ears. It rolled across the room again, and unwound itself.

"Pooh," said Piglet nervously.

"Yes?" said one of the chairs.

"Where are we?"

"I'm not quite sure," said the chair.

"Are we – are we in Owl's House?"

"I think so, because we were just going to have tea, and we hadn't had it."

"Oh!" said Piglet. "Well, did Owl *always* have a letter-box in his ceiling?"

"Has he?"

"Yes, look."

"I can't," said Pooh. "I'm face downwards under something, and that, Piglet, is a very bad position for looking at ceilings."

"Well, he has, Pooh."

"Perhaps he's changed it," said Pooh. "Just for a change."

There was a disturbance behind the table in the other corner of the room, and Owl was with them again.

"Ah, Piglet," said Owl, looking very much annoyed; "where's Pooh?"

"I'm not quite sure," said Pooh.

Owl turned at his voice, and frowned at as much of Pooh as he could see.

"Pooh," said Owl severely, "did *you* do that?"

"No," said Pooh humbly. "I don't *think* so."

"Then who did?"

"I think it was the wind," said Piglet. "I think your house has blown down."

"Oh, is that it? I thought it was Pooh."

"No," said Pooh.

"If it was the wind," said Owl, considering the matter, "then it wasn't Pooh's fault. No blame can be attached to him." With these kind words he flew up to look at his new ceiling.

"Piglet!" called Pooh in a loud whisper.

Piglet leant down to him.

"Yes, Pooh?"

"*What* did he say was attached to me?"

"He said he didn't blame you."

"Oh! I thought he meant — Oh, I see."

"Owl," said Piglet, "come down and help Pooh."

Owl, who was admiring his letter-box, flew down again. Together they pushed and pulled at the arm-chair, and in a little while Pooh came out from underneath, and was able to look round him again.

"Well!" said Owl. "This is a nice state of things!"

"What are we going to do, Pooh? Can you think of anything?" asked Piglet.

"Well, I *had* just thought of something," said Pooh. "It was just a little thing I thought of." And he began to sing:

> I lay on my chest
> And I thought it best
> To pretend I was having an evening rest;
> I lay on my tum
> And I tried to hum
> But nothing particular seemed to come.
> My face was flat
> On the floor, and that

Is all very well for an acrobat;
But it doesn't seem fair
To a Friendly Bear
To stiffen him out with a basket-chair.
And a sort of sqoze
Which grows and grows
Is not too nice for his poor old nose,
And a sort of squch
Is much too much
For his neck and his mouth and his ears and such.

"That was all," said Pooh.

Owl coughed in an unadmiring sort of way, and said that, if Pooh was sure that *was* all, they could now give their minds to the Problem of Escape.

"Because," said Owl, "we can't go out by what used to be the front door. Something's fallen on it."

"But how else *can* you go out?" asked Piglet anxiously.

"That is the Problem, Piglet, to which I am asking Pooh to give his mind."

Pooh sat on the floor which had once been a wall, and gazed up at the ceiling which had once been another wall, with a front door in it which had once been a front door, and tried to give his mind to it.

"Could you fly up to the letter-box with Piglet on your back?" he asked.

"No," said Piglet quickly. "He couldn't."

Owl explained about the Necessary Dorsal Muscles. He had explained this to Pooh and Christopher Robin once before, and had been waiting ever since for a chance to do it again, because it is a thing which you can easily explain twice before anybody knows what you are talking about.

"Because you see, Owl, if we could get Piglet into the letter-box, he might squeeze through the place where the letters come, and climb down the tree and run for help."

Piglet said hurriedly that he had been getting bigger lately, and couldn't *possibly*, much as he would like to, and Owl said that he had had his letter-box made bigger lately in case he got bigger letters, so perhaps Piglet *might*, and Piglet said, "But you said the necessary you-know-whats *wouldn't*," and Owl said, "No, they *won't*, so it's no good thinking about it," and Piglet said, "Then we'd better think of something else," and began to at once.

But Pooh's mind had gone back to the day when he had saved Piglet from the flood, and everybody had admired him so much; and as that didn't often happen, he thought he would like it to happen again. And suddenly, just as it had come before, an idea came to him.

"Owl," said Pooh. "I have thought of something."

"Astute and Helpful Bear," said Owl.

Pooh looked proud at being called a stout and helpful bear, and said modestly that he just happened to think of it. You tied a piece of string to Piglet, and you flew up to the letter-box, with the other end in your beak, and you pushed it through the wire and brought it down to the floor, and you and Pooh pulled hard at this end, and Piglet went slowly up at the other end. And there you were.

"And there Piglet is," said Owl. "If the string doesn't break."

"Supposing it does?" asked Piglet, really wanting to know.

"Then we try another piece of string."

This was not very comforting to Piglet, because however many pieces of string they tried pulling up with, it would always be the same him coming down; but still, it did seem the only thing to do. So with one last look back in his mind at all the happy hours he had spent in the Forest *not* being pulled up to the ceiling by a piece of string, Piglet nodded bravely at Pooh and said that it was a Very Clever pup-pup-pup Clever pup-pup Plan.

"It won't break," whispered Pooh comfortingly, "because you're a Small Animal, and I'll stand underneath, and if you save us all, it will be a Very Grand Thing to talk about afterwards, and perhaps I'll make up a Song, and people will say 'It was so grand what Piglet did that a Respectful Pooh Song was made about it!'"

Piglet felt much better after this, and when everything was ready, and he found himself slowly going up to the ceiling, he was so proud that he would have called out "Look at *me*!" if he hadn't been afraid that Pooh and Owl would let go of their end of the string and look at him.

"Up we go!" said Pooh cheerfully.

"The ascent is proceeding as expected," said Owl helpfully. Soon it was over. Piglet opened the letter-box and climbed in. Then, having untied himself, he began to squeeze into the slit, through which in the old days when front doors *were* front doors, many an unexpected letter that WOL had written to himself, had come slipping.

He squeezed and he sqoze, and then with one last squze he was out. Happy and excited he turned round to squeak a last message to the prisoners.

"It's all right," he called through the letter-box. "Your tree is blown right over, Owl, and there's a branch across the door, but Christopher Robin and I can move it, and we'll bring a rope for Pooh, and I'll go and tell him now, and I can climb down quite easily, I mean it's dangerous but I can do it all right, and Christopher Robin and I will be back in about half an hour. Good-bye, Pooh!" And without waiting to hear Pooh's answering "Good-bye, and thank you, Piglet," he was off.

"Half an hour," said Owl, settling himself comfortably. "That will just give me time to finish that story I was telling you about my Uncle Robert – a portrait of whom you see underneath you. Now let me see, where was I? Oh, yes. It was on just such a blusterous day as this that my Uncle Robert —"

Pooh closed his eyes.

WIND ON THE HILL

No one can tell me,
Nobody knows,
Where the wind comes from,
Where the wind goes.

SOLITUDE

I have a house where I go
    When there's too many people,
I have a house where I go
    Where no one can be;
I have a house where I go,
Where nobody ever says "No"
Where no one says anything – so
    There is no one but me.

An Enchanted Place

Christopher Robin was going away. Nobody knew why he was going; nobody knew where he was going; indeed, nobody even knew why he knew that Christopher Robin *was* going away. But somehow or other everybody in the Forest felt that it was happening at last. Even Smallest-of-all, a friend-and-relation of Rabbit's who thought he had once seen Christopher Robin's foot, but couldn't be quite sure because perhaps it was something else, even S. of A. told himself that Things were going to be Different; and Late and Early, two other friends-and-relations, said, "Well, Early?" and "Well, Late?" to each other in such a hopeless sort of way that it really didn't seem any good waiting for the answer.

One day when he felt that he couldn't wait any longer, Rabbit brained out a Notice, and this is what it said:

"Notice a meeting of everybody will meet at the House at Pooh Corner to pass a Rissolution By Order Keep to the Left Signed Rabbit."

He had to write this out two or three times before he could get the rissolution to look like what he thought it was going to when he began to spell it; but, when at last it was finished, he took it round to everybody and read it out to them. And they all said they would come.

"Well," said Eeyore that afternoon, when he saw them all walking up to his house, "this *is* a surprise. Am *I* asked too?"

"Don't mind Eeyore," whispered Rabbit to Pooh. "I told him all about it this morning."

Everybody said "How-do-you-do" to Eeyore, and Eeyore said that he didn't, not to notice, and then they sat down; and as soon as they were all sitting down, Rabbit stood up again.

"We all know why we're here," he said, "but I have asked my friend Eyore —"

"That's Me," said Eeyore. "Grand."

"I have asked him to Propose a Rissolution." And he sat down again. "Now then, Eeyore," he said.

"Don't Bustle me," said Eeyore, getting up slowly. "Don't now-then me." He took a piece of paper from behind his ear, and unfolded it. "Nobody knows anything about this," he went on. "This is a Surprise." He coughed in an important way, and began again: "What-nots and Etceteras, before I begin, or perhaps I should say, before I end, I have a piece of Poetry to read to you. Hitherto – hitherto – a long word meaning – well, you'll see what it means directly – hitherto, as I was saying, all the Poetry in the Forest has been written by Pooh, a Bear with a Pleasing Manner but a Positively Startling Lack of Brain. The Poem which I am now about to read to you was written by Eeyore, o Myself, in a Quiet Moment. If somebody wil take Roo's bull's eye away from him, and wak up Owl, we shall all be able to enjoy it. I call it – POEM."

   This was it:

Christopher Robin is going.
At least I think he is.
Where?
Nobody knows.
But he is going –
I mean he goes
(*To rhyme with "knows"*)
Do we care?
(*To rhyme with "where"*)
We do
Very much.
(*I haven't got a rhyme for that "is" in the second line yet.*
Bother.)
(*Now I haven't got a rhyme for bother. Bother.*)
Those two bothers will have to rhyme with each other
Buther.
The fact is this is more difficult
than I thought,
I ought –
(*Very good indeed*)
I ought
To begin again,
But it is easier
To stop.
Christopher Robin, good-bye,
I
(*Good*)
I
And all your friends
Sends –
I mean all your friend
Send –
(*Very awkward this, it keeps going wrong.*)
Well, anyhow, we send
Our love
END.

"If anybody wants to clap," said Eeyore when he had read this, "now is the time to do it."

They all clapped.

"Thank you," said Eeyore. "Unexpected and gratifying, if a little lacking in Smack."

Pooh

WOL

Piglet

"It's much better than mine," said Pooh admiringly, and he really thought it was.

"Well," explained Eeyore modestly, "it was meant to be."

Rabbit

eOR

"The rissolution," said Rabbit, "is that we all sign it, and take it to Christopher Robin."

So it was signed
PooH, WOL, PIGLET,
EOR, RABBIT,
KANGA, BLOT,
SMUDGE,

and they all went off to Christopher Robin's house with it.

"Hallo, everybody," said Christopher Robin – "Hallo, Pooh."

They all said "Hallo," and felt awkward and unhappy suddenly, because it was a sort of good-bye they were saying, and they didn't want to think about it. So they stood around, and waited for somebody else to speak, and they nudged each other, and said "Go on," and gradually Eeyore was nudged to the front, and the others crowded behind him.

"What is it, Eeyore?" asked Christopher Robin.

Eeyore swished his tail from side to side, so as to encourage himself, and began.

"Christopher Robin," he said, "we've come to say – to give you – it's called –

written by – but we've all – because we've heard, I mean we all know – well, you see, it's – we – you – well, that, to put it as shortly as possible, is what it is." He turned round angrily on the others and said, "Everybody crowds round so in this Forest. There's no Space. I never saw a more Spreading lot of animals in my life, and all in the wrong places. Can't you *see* that Christopher Robin wants to be alone? I'm going." And he humped off.

Not quite knowing why, the others began edging away, and when Christopher Robin had finished reading POEM, and was looking up to say "Thank you," only Pooh was left.

"It's a comforting sort of thing to have," said Christopher Robin, folding up the paper, and putting it in his pocket. "Come on, Pooh," and he walked off quickly.

"Where are we going?" said Pooh, hurrying after him, and wondering whether it was to be an Explore or a What-shall-I-do-about-you-know-what.

"Nowhere," said Christopher Robin.

So they began going there, and after they had walked a little way Christopher Robin said:

"What do you like doing best in the world, Pooh?"

"Well," said Pooh, "what I like best —" and then he had to stop and think. Because although Eating Honey *was* a very good thing to do, there was a moment just before you began to eat it which was better than when you were, but he didn't know what it was called. And then he thought that being with Christopher Robin was a very good thing to do, and having Piglet near was a very friendly thing to have; and so, when he had thought it all out, he said, "What I like best in the whole world is Me and Piglet going to see You, and You saying, 'What about a little something?' and Me saying, 'Well, I shouldn't mind a little something, should you, Piglet,' and it being a hummy sort of day outside, and birds singing."

"I like that too," said Christopher Robin, "but what I like *doing* best is Nothing."

"How do you do Nothing?" asked Pooh, after he had wondered for a long time.

"Well, it's when people call out at you just as you're going off to do it, 'What are you going to do, Christopher Robin?' and you say 'Oh, nothing,' and then you go and do it."

"Oh, I see," said Pooh.

"This is a nothing sort of thing that we're doing now."

"Oh, I see," said Pooh again.

"It means just going along, listening to all the things you can't hear, and not bothering."

"Oh!" said Pooh.

They walked on, thinking of This and That, and by-and-by they came to an enchanted place on the very top of the Forest called Galleons Lap, which is sixty-something trees in a circle; and Christopher Robin knew that it was enchanted because nobody had ever been able to count whether it was sixty-three or sixty-four, not even when he tied a piece of string round each tree after he had counted it. Being enchanted, its floor was not like the floor of the Forest, gorse and bracken and heather, but close-set grass, quiet and smooth and green. It was the only place in the Forest where you could sit down carelessly, without getting up again almost at once and looking for somewhere else. Sitting there they could see the whole world spread out until it reached the sky, and whatever there was all the world over was with them in Galleons Lap.

Suddenly Christopher Robin began to tell Pooh about some of the things: People called Kings and Queens and something called Factors, and a place called Europe, and an island in the middle of the sea where no ships came, and how you make a Suction Pump (if you want to), and when Knights were Knighted, and what comes from Brazil. And Pooh, his back against one of the sixty-something trees, and his paws folded in front of him, said "Oh!" and "I don't know," and thought how wonderful it would be to have a Real Brain which could tell you things. And by-and-by Christopher Robin came to an end of the things, and was silent, and he sat there looking out over the world, and wishing it wouldn't stop.

But Pooh was thinking too, and he said suddenly to Christopher Robin:

"Is it a very Grand thing to be an Afternoon, what you said?"

"A what?" said Christopher Robin lazily, as he listened to something else.

"On a horse?" explained Pooh.

"A Knight?"

"Oh, was that it?" said Pooh. "I thought it was a — Is it as Grand as a King and Factors and all the other things you said?"

"Well, it's not as grand as a King," said Christopher Robin, and then, as Pooh seemed disappointed, he added quickly, "but it's grander than Factors."

"Could a Bear be one?"

"Of course he could!" said Christopher Robin. "I'll make you one." And he took a stick and touched Pooh on the shoulder, and said, "Rise, Sir Pooh de Bear, most faithful of all my Knights."

So Pooh rose and sat down and said "Thank you," which is the proper thing to say when you have been made a Knight, and he went into a dream again, in which he and Sir Pump and Sir Brazil and Factors lived together with a horse, and were faithful knights (all except Factors, who looked after the horse) to Good King Christopher Robin . . .

and every now and then he shook his head, and said to himself, "I'm not getting it right." Then he began to think of all the things Christopher Robin would want to tell him when he came back from wherever he was going to, and how muddling it would be for a Bear of Very Little Brain to try and get them right in his mind. "So, perhaps," he said sadly to himself, "Christopher Robin won't tell me any more," and he wondered if being a Faithful Knight meant that you just went on being faithful without being told things.

Then, suddenly again, Christopher Robin, who was still looking at the world with his chin in his hands, called out "Pooh!"

"Yes?" said Pooh.

"When I'm – when — Pooh!"

"Yes, Christopher Robin?"

"I'm not going to do Nothing any more."

"Never again?"

"Well, not so much. They don't let you."

Pooh waited for him to go on, but he was silent again.

"Yes, Christopher Robin?" said Pooh helpfully.

"Pooh, when I'm – *you* know – when I'm *not* doing Nothing, will you come up here sometimes?"

"Just Me?"

"Yes, Pooh."

"Will you be here too?"

"Yes, Pooh, I will be really. I *promise* I will be, Pooh."

"That's good," said Pooh.

"Pooh, *promise* you won't forget about me, ever. Not even when I'm a hundred."

Pooh thought for a little.

"How old shall *I* be then?"

"Ninety-nine."

Pooh nodded.

"I promise," he said.

Still with his eyes on the world Christopher Robin put out a hand and felt for Pooh's paw.

"Pooh," said Christopher Robin earnestly, "if I – if I'm not quite —" he stopped and tried again – "Pooh, *whatever* happens, you *will* understand, won't you?"

"Understand what?"

"Oh, nothing." He laughed and jumped to his feet. "Come on!"

"Where?" said Pooh.

"Anywhere," said Christopher Robin.

So they went off together. But wherever they go, and whatever happens to them on the way, in that enchanted place on the top of the Forest a little boy and his Bear will always be playing.

The Charcoal-Burner

The charcoal-burner has tales to tell.
He lives in the Forest,
Alone in the Forest;
He sits in the Forest,
Alone in the Forest.
And the sun comes slanting between the trees,
And rabbits come up, and they give him good-morning,
And rabbits come up and say, "Beautiful morning"...
And the moon swings clear of the tall black trees,
And owls fly over and wish him good-night,
Quietly over to wish him good-night ...

And he sits and thinks of the things they know,
He and the Forest, alone together –
The springs that come and the summers that go,
Autumn dew on bracken and heather,
The drip of the Forest beneath the snow ...

All the things they have seen,
All the things they have heard:
An April sky swept clean and the song of a bird . . .

Oh, the charcoal-burner has tales to tell!
And he lives in the Forest and knows us well.

THE FRIEND

There are lots and lots of people who are always asking things,
Like Dates and Pounds-and-ounces and the names of funny Kings,
And the answer's either Sixpence or A Hundred Inches Long.
And I know they'll think me silly if I get the answer wrong.

So Pooh and I go whispering, and Pooh looks very bright,
And says, "Well, *I* say sixpence, but I don't suppose I'm right."
And then it doesn't matter what the answer ought to be,
'Cos if he's right, I'm Right, and if he's wrong, it isn't Me.